P9-DEH-115

N B
16 . 9 . 01 .

The Epigrams of
OSCAR
WILDE

The Epigrams of
OSCAR
WILDE

EDITED BY
ALVIN REDMAN

INTRODUCTION BY
VYVYAN HOLLAND

SENATE

The Epigrams of Oscar Wilde

First published in 1952 by Alvin Redman Ltd, London

This edition published in 1996 by Senate,
an imprint of Senate Press Limited,
34 York Street, Twickenham,
Middlesex TW1 3LJ, United Kingdom

Compilation © Alvin Redman 1952
Cover design © Senate Press Limited 1996

5 7 9 10 8 6 4

All rights reserved. No part of this publication may be
reproduced, stored in a retrieval system or transmitted,
in any form or by any means, electronic, mechanical,
photocopying, recording or otherwise, without the prior
permission of the copyright owners.

ISBN 1 85958 516 7

Printed and bound in Guernsey by
The Guernsey Press Co. Ltd

I knew him well and am proud to have been his friend. He has become the symbolic figure of his age, which he summed up completely. He made dying Victorianism laugh at itself and what serious reformers had laboured for years to accomplish he did in a moment with the flash of an epigram; gaily, with humour and wit for his weapons.

RICHARD LE GALLIENE.*

* From " The Romantic 90's ",
published by Putnam & Co., Ltd., 1925, re-issued 1952.

PREFACE

THE following collection of sayings by Oscar Wilde has been taken from his published works, lectures, letters, and fragmentary records of his conversation left by his many biographers.

The title is one of convenience. It was suggested by an incident which occurred whilst Oscar Wilde was in prison. Lord Haldane who felt, very strongly, that Wilde's sentence was a savage one, visited him in his cell. He suggested that Wilde should use his leisure time in writing a considerable work. Wilde jocularly said that he was preparing a book of table epigrams.

Wilde's writings are generally considered to be mainly autobiographical, and I trust that the brief notes to the various categories will be of assistance to the reader in forming a separate opinion of Oscar Wilde.

I wish to place on record my sincere gratitude to Mr. Vyvyan Holland and Mr. H. Montgomery Hyde for their kindly interest and gracious co-operation in the compilation of this volume, and for the right to reproduce copyright material.

Mr. Vyvyan Holland, Oscar Wilde's son, has contributed a valuable and interesting introduction and by his kindness in reading the proofs has ensured the authenticity of the material.

Mr. H. Montgomery Hyde is a foremost authority on Oscar Wilde, and a point of interest is that when he was at Magdalen College, Oxford, he occupied the rooms overlooking the Cherwell, that many years before had been Oscar Wilde's. Mr. H. Montgomery Hyde's book, "The Trials of Oscar Wilde", is a classic of its kind and his reconstruction of the Trials necessitated lengthy and careful research. I am especially indebted to him for his valuable advice and assistance that have made possible the compilation of the Trials section of this volume.

My grateful acknowledgments are also due to the many others who by their kind co-operation have assisted in the preparation of this book.

ALVIN REDMAN

CONTENTS

INTRODUCTION

To the present generation Oscar Wilde's literary reputation rests mainly on *The Importance of Being Earnest, Lady Windermere's Fan, The Picture of Dorian Gray,* and *De Profundis.* The large number of essays, criticisms, lectures and reviews which he wrote during his comparatively brief literary life are little known to the general reading public.

The chief essays are contained in *Intentions,* and *The Soul of Man Under Socialism.* These show such deep thought and insight into human nature that it is difficult to believe that they were written by the same hand that wrote *The Importance of Being Earnest* and *Lady Windermere's Fan,* with their delightfully superficial cynicism and wit. I sometimes think that this very cynicism was assumed in order to conceal the more serious side of his mind.

Oscar Wilde's criticisms, lectures and reviews are even less widely read than his essays. Indeed, much of this part of his work might have been irretrievably lost if it had not been rescued and reprinted in the first collected edition of his works published in 1908. It is an unfortunate fact that some of the writings of even the most eminent authors may become lost for years, and sometimes for ever, because they have appeared in weekly or monthly periodicals which, after a few years, survive only in one or two Reference Libraries, where they soon sink into oblivion.

So many of my father's contemporaries have recorded their recollections of his conversations in their reminiscences that it has become a formidable task in itself to collect all the sayings with which he has been credited. And it is an even more formidable task to decide which of the sayings really did originate with him. It is the fate of all celebrities who acquire a reputation for wit to have remarks attributed to them which they would indignantly repudiate if they were alive to do so.

In the case of Oscar Wilde, this fate has been carried a step further, as whole books have been attributed to him which were written long after his death. Glaring examples of this are a "masque" entitled *For Love of the King*, for which Wilde wrote a synopsis only, but which was published later as a complete play, a blatant forgery published in 1922 and later the subject of a court case, and a book of reports of rather naïve conversations with a medium at a series of spiritualistic séances at which he is supposed to have appeared. And there are other books to which unscrupulous people have appended his name, in an effort, presumably, to increase their sales.

The English laws of slander and libel allow people to say anything they like about the dead, however scandalously untrue it may be and however much it may distress surviving relatives. And, paradoxically, under our copyright laws, a literary executor cannot stop the publication of a spurious book unless he is dishonest enough to admit that it is genuine and claim the copyright himself!

Mr. Alvin Redman has done a service to literature in collecting Oscar Wilde's more important epigrammatic writings and utterances into one volume. It is noteworthy that he has ignored all the spurious works attributed to Wilde. He has acquitted himself very well of his difficult task, which can only have been achieved by the most patient and painstaking research. He has chosen for his conversational quotations only those that are well authenticated as coming from unimpeachable sources, and the quotations from the published works have been selected with discrimination and discretion.

VYVYAN HOLLAND.

THE SUPREME CONVERSATIONALIST

FIFTY years after the death of Oscar Wilde the conversation which expressed his genius has become a legend. Conversation is an ephemeral art, and as the autumn breezes blow the brown leaves to eternity, the spring green freshness becomes only a memory. So it is with Oscar Wilde. In the conversational quality of his writings, and in the many biographies he has inspired, fragmentary record of his talk remains; but the musical intonation of his voice and all the magic of his personality have gone for ever.

The personality of Wilde is a significant feature in an attempted analysis of his power of speech. Laurence Housman, who knew Wilde, is one who maintains that as a personality Wilde was more remarkable than as a writer, and in his introduction to *Echo de Paris* Housman says: " . . . the impression left on me . . . is that Oscar Wilde was incomparably the most accomplished talker I had ever met. The smooth, flowing utterance, sedate and self-possessed, oracular in tone, whimsical in substance, carried on without halt, or hesitation, or change of word, with the queer zest of a man perfect at the game, and conscious that, for the moment at least, he was back at his old form again; this, combined with the pleasure, infectious to his listeners, of finding himself once more in a group of friends whose view of his downfall was not the world's view, made memorable to others besides myself a reunion more happily prolonged than this selected portion of it would indicate."

Two of Wilde's biographers, who undoubtedly speak from personal knowledge, have paid tribute to the charm of Wilde's personality. Robert Harborough Sherard, one of Wilde's closest friends, had good reason to remember the enlivening effect of his influence. Sherard was of a melancholy turn of mind and at one time contemplated suicide. He discussed his affairs with Wilde and was rescued from his despondency by the sparkling philosophy of Wilde's conversation. Sherard records in his book

17

Oscar Wilde : " The man who was afterwards branded as a corrupter of youth exerted in me, as a young man, an influence altogether beneficial. If he had taught me nothing but the great value and happiness of life, I should still owe him an unpayable debt, for my disposition tended to that *tædium vitæ* which makes existence pure misery."

Sherard gives us another description of Wilde's enchantment, this time, he assures us, " written by a man who was not a friend."

" . . . as he proceeded he was caught by the pathos of his own words, his beautiful voice trembled with emotion, his eyes swam with tears; and then suddenly, by a swift, indescribably brilliant, whimsical touch, a swallow wing flash on the waters of eloquence, the tone changed, and rippled with laughter, bringing with it his audience, relieved, delighted and bubbling with uncontrollable merriment."

This was Wilde towards the end of his life and the tears were for the pathos of his own tragedy as he recounted the steps of his downfall. In fairness to Wilde he possessed such a sympathetic nature that he was probably viewing the story objectively, and no doubt, he would have evinced the same emotion in describing a similar tragedy in which he himself played no part. In point of fact, Wilde bore the many indignities which were heaped upon him after his downfall with fortitude, and certainly without displaying malice or ill-feeling.

The other biographer, Frank Harris, who knew Wilde intimately, wrote : " I miss no one so much as I miss Oscar Wilde. . . . I would rather have him back now than almost anyone I have ever met. I have known more heroic souls and some deeper souls; souls more keenly alive to ideals of duty and generosity; but I have known no more charming, no more quickening, no more delightful spirit . . . The most charming man I have ever met was assuredly Oscar Wilde. I do not believe that in all the realms of death there is a more fascinating or delightful companion."

All who met Wilde were charmed and he exerted his influence over an extremely wide range of individuals. A notable testimony to Wilde's good nature was paid by Dr. Winnington

18

Ingram, late Bishop of London, who said: "I knew Wilde and in spite of his one great vice—which was surely pathological—I never met a man who united in himself so many lovable and Christian virtues."

Even Wilde's enemies were unable to resist the spell of his presence, and probably the best example of his fascination even over those who disliked him, is an incident which occurred when Wilde was lunching with Lord Alfred Douglas in the Café Royal. A few tables away sat the Marquess of Queensberry who was undoubtedly Wilde's most bitter enemy, and he stared across with undisguised loathing. Douglas went over to his father and asked him to join them. Queensberry refused with disgust, but eventually he grudgingly consented to the introduction. He sat down determined to evince his intense dislike, but within a matter of minutes he was laughing boisterously and was completely under the spell of Wilde's personality.

They talked until well into the afternoon and Queensberry was loath to leave, so well was he enjoying the conversation. He was charmed and delighted, and later wrote a letter to his son expressing his pleasure at the meeting, saying that Wilde was a wonderful man and wonderful talker.

Many other instances could be quoted of Wilde meeting people who were positively antagonistic towards him, and yet within a very short space of time they had forgotten their prejudices and were heartily enjoying his company.

Oscar Wilde possessed a keen understanding of human nature, with the result that in whatever stratum of society he found himself, he was able to exert his charm with success. Workmen, fishermen, actors, politicians, lawyers, scientists, women, children, they were all captivated by his conversation. Wilde's friends were many and varied, although it is interesting to note that not many were fellow-writers.

Wilde's personality burned like the flames of a beautiful dancing fire: gay, wayward, and warming. But beneath the gaiety there was a kindly, if complex, nature, and though the flames warmed they never burned those they touched. André Gide confirms the depth of Wilde's apparent surface charm and he once said: "Though I do not wish to flatter Wilde, I am aware that in spite of his many defects, I never for a moment doubted his greatness . . . People did not always realize how much truth, wisdom and seriousness were concealed under the mask of a jester."

An instance of Wilde's friendliness occurred when Wilde was in Reading Gaol. Wilde was ill in the prison hospital, and an appeal for his early release was pending. The Home Office representatives visited Wilde to consider his case. Wilde knew of the appeal and although ill was in buoyant spirits at the possibility of an early release. They found him, sitting on his bed, surrounded by an enthralled and delighted audience of fellow-prisoners.

The Home Office representatives had expected to find a very different person to the gay, sparkling conversationalist they saw. In consequence, the appeal failed. When Wilde heard the result of the appeal he suffered a relapse, and had the officials seen him then they might have reported differently.

Wilde's was a nature that felt the sufferings of others. The genuineness of his sympathy is exemplified by many acts of generosity to those in need. He lived in a world of gestures, and an interesting insight into this side of his nature is given by Edgar Saltus, who included the following in his book *Oscar Wilde*.

" Afterwards we drove back to Chelsea. It was a vile night, bleak and bitter. On alighting, a man came up to me. He wore a short jacket which he opened. From neck to waist he was bare. I gave him a shilling. Then came the rebuke. With entire simplicity Wilde took off his overcoat and put it about the man.

" But the simplicity seemed to me too Hugoesque and I said : ' Why don't you ask him in to dinner? '

" Wilde gestured. ' Dinner is not a feast, it is a ceremony.' "

It has been said that Wilde talked for effect—but to what effect! His whole manner was one of self-confidence and yet he was seldom condescending. He was essentially eccentric and an individualist, but behind the flamboyant façade there existed a genuine understanding of other points of view besides his own. Anna de Brémont, reporting on Wilde's American trip, illustrated in the following how Wilde was happier sharing the views at a dinner-table than making the dogmatic statements of a lecturer. " He shone to far greater and better advantage amid these surroundings than he did on the lecture platform. There was a dignity and graciousness in his manner that blinded one to his eccentric appearance."

Wilde had many faults but it is obvious that they were not apparent on meeting him. In his early days, in London particularly, he was extravagantly eccentric in dress and mannerisms, but all to good purpose, for he was his own publicity agent, and a very effective one indeed. He viewed the antagonism shown towards his eccentricities with benign complacency. Indeed, he once offered as advice the following remark, " If you wish for reputation and fame in the world and success during your life-time, you are right to take every opportunity of advertising yourself, you remember the Latin saying, Fame springs from one's own house." In support of this statement he made a particular point of being seen on important social occasions, and on " first nights " before the rise of the curtain, he would appear in various parts of the house; his outlandish figure seemed to pop up everywhere, the boxes, the stalls, the dress-circle, radiating an air of excitement and good humour.

In appearance, at the zenith of his fame, he was a tall bulky figure, with a large, pale, clean-shaven face surmounted by an abundance of long, dark-brown hair. Success had coarsened his features. His cheeks were heavy, his lips sensual, his teeth had lost their whiteness, but the harmony of his face was still maintained by the high forehead, kindly mouth, firm jaw, and eloquent eyes. Eyes which were one moment twinkling with merriment and the next were sombre and sad.

He dressed meticulously in the fashion of the day, wearing a button-hole, chosen with care, and carrying a walking-stick, also carefully selected, from his large collection.

Despite the correctness of his dress Wilde was an unusual figure, with his dark, flowing hair, and glowing eyes accentuating the pallor of his cheeks. At first sight he was not attractive, but his smile predominated his features and the obviously genuine humour which lurked behind his utterances dispelled suspicion, and made dislike impossible.

When he spoke the charm was complete, for his voice, apart from his words, was exceptionally pleasing. It was modulated, musical, rounded, and Wilde, aware of its power of enchantment, used it with full dramatic effect.

Few remain of those who heard his talk, but his many biographers are unanimous in acclaiming Wilde as the supreme conversationalist. The descriptions are many and varied, and Wilde himself, in the character of Lord Henry Wotton in *The Picture of Dorian Gray,* has left a most apt description, by example, of his conversation. He describes Lord Wotton's talk in the following short extract :

" He played with the idea, grew wilful; tossed it into the air and transformed it; let it escape and recaptured it; made it iridescent with fancy, and winged it with paradox. The praise of folly, as he went on soared into a philosophy, and Philosophy herself became young, and catching the mad music of Pleasure wearing, one might fancy, her wine-stained robe and wreath of ivy, danced like a Bacchante over the hills of Life, and mocked the slow Silenus for being sober. Facts spread before her like frightened forest things. Her white feet trod the huge press at which the wise Omar sits, till the seething grape-juice rose round her bare limbs in waves of purple bubbles, or crawled in red foam over the vat's black, dripping, sloping sides. It was an extraordinary improvisation."

This was Wilde himself, buoyantly guiding the narrative through many bright bejewelled caverns until he reached the daylight of his story, and then smilingly turning back to find new adventures for his words.

Spellbound like his audience he was an entranced spectator of his own dazzling eloquence, and indeed, Wilde said : " To become a spectator of one's own life is to escape the suffering of life." He viewed his life objectively as a work of art, and used his conversation as a means of expressing the tremendous creative urge within himself. His talk revealed every facet of his glittering, bizarre personality, his wit, his scholarship, his quick, penetrating intellect, his delight in the use of decorative, high-sounding words, his love of the ornate and picturesque, his vanity and naïve love of flattery, and, lastly, his tolerant good nature.

Here was the dilettante, the amateur genius, who regarded his life as being infinitely more important than his works, the life-lover who lived for the sound of his own voice.

Oscar Wilde made every conversation an occasion. His talk was the "rage" of London society and his arrival caused a hush of expectancy. He never disappointed. He seemed to sense immediately the mood and intelligence of his audience, and moulded his talk to suit the company.

Sometimes he was gay, witty, startling, and his talk was a froth of light-hearted irresponsibilities. At other times, he held his listeners enthralled as he recounted an engrossing but improbable narrative, embellishing his account with impromptu decorations. He spoke in parables, told anecdotes, fairy-stories, maintaining the same degree of fascination whether his talk prompted laughter or tears. Never at loss for a word, a phrase, or a flashback of memory, his talk flowed on with the fluent, accomplished ease of an actor perfect in his part. His amazing fertility of intellect produced a new and unexpected turn in his talk, or a new story, almost without a pause. There was but the momentary closure of his eyelids and in that brief flicker of time a new picture flashed across his mind, whilst without effort, his rounded modulated voice brought it vividly to life.

His fund of knowledge seemed inexhaustible, for what he didn't know, he invented. He touched upon everything with the same sureness, supremely confident. On one occasion at the dinner-table he was taken up on his boast that he could talk on any subject, immediately and spontaneously. There was a moment's silence and then a voice said: "The Queen." Almost before the words were out of the speaker's mouth Wilde turned and said softly: "The Queen is not a subject."

His pictures, painted in words, were glowing, colourful, works of art, with a deep underlying meaning, but it is impossible to visualize the complete tapestry of his conversation in which his wit, his stories, his fairy-tale improbabilities, and intellectual brilliance mingled so effectively.

Wilde's conversation was as varied as his writings and on examining his works one can find in each a different illustration of his talk.

Oscar Wilde's poems, with the exception of *The Ballad of Reading Gaol,* and about half a dozen others, are not considered to be an important part of his writings, but at least they were his first introduction to print in volume form.

Poems, his first book, is a collection of his work before and after *Ravenna,* the Newdigate Prize Poem, and it is the story of his boyhood. On every page Wilde gives indications of the perennial youthfulness to which he was to cling all his life, and which was always a predominant feature of his personality.

He tells of his travels in Italy and Greece, his first love-affair, and his admiration for the Catholic faith. The book contains the outpourings of the knowledge and learning, which he had stored in his restless, questing mind.

In later life Wilde wrote with a feverish impetuosity, drawing upon his creative urge with an impatience that at times became carelessness. In *Poems,* this same impetuosity is displayed, but on this first occasion he draws upon the works and ideas of others —Rossetti, Swinburne, Milton, Marlowe, Dante, Keats, Browning, are among those from whom he borrowed.

Poems is the work of the young scholar delighting in his classical learning and his ability to write beautiful phrases and descriptions, and we can recognize that joyous spirit of youth which remained as a characteristic of Wilde's emotional outlook.

Wilde's " fairy-tale " talk is to be found in his books *The Happy Prince and other Tales* and *A House of Pomegranates.* In these Wilde speaks with the voice of Hans Christian Andersen, and *The Happy Prince* story in particular is beautiful and touching.

A House of Pomegranates was written a year later and although there is still a ring of Hans Andersen, the tales are not intended for children. They are haunting in their beauty, and Wilde introduces the elaborate and decorative effect which is so essentially his own. These curious and beautiful tales are a unique contribution to English literature and are perfect examples of the chimerical quality of Wilde's talk.

At times Wilde spoke in parables, and his *Poems in Prose* is a case in point. The fairy-tale quality is still present, but there, the similarity to his other writings ends. They are amongst the most beautiful and wonderful things that Wilde wrote, although it is said they were even more wonderful in his original conversation at the dinner-table, but in their present form they are exquisite masterpieces.

One can well imagine his listeners becoming spellbound by this style of talk; perfect sentences, spoken without hesitation and with flowing, confident ease.

Wilde's only novel, *The Picture of Dorian Gray*, is of particular importance in describing his conversation. It has been termed " the first French novel to be written in the English language " and this description has become almost a subtitle; certainly it is unlike any other novel written in the English language.

The plot, no doubt, owes something to Balzac's *Le Peau de Chagrin*, in which a piece of skin shrinks with each wish of its possessor, for in a similar way, in *Dorian Gray*, a portrait of a young man ages and becomes lined with each sin committed by its subject. The treatment of the story, however, is essentially Wilde's, and bears the unmistakable stamp of his bizarre personality, his love of the elaborate and ornate, and his delight in the unreal.

More important than the story is the fact that in the character of Lord Henry Wotton is a self-portrait of Wilde as a light-hearted conversationalist. Into *Dorian Gray* he poured his personality, his ideas, his opinions and his wit, and the book contains the largest collection of his epigrams, aphorisms and paradoxes, many of which appear later in his plays and other works.

Perhaps the most amazing features of Wilde's talk was his ability to invent a story to suit perfectly the mood of the moment. It is surprising, therefore, that so few of his stories were published. Mr. Sherard records that Oscar Wilde was often visited, whilst in bed, by his brother William who was a journalist. He was seeking stories and Oscar obliged by reeling off as many as six stories in succession, effortlessly and without apparent thought. Stories teemed from his brain in the same way during his conversation and, unfortunately, Wilde found them so easy to invent that he did not deign to set pen to paper, but many of them found their way into print, suffering on the way, under the guidance of William. From all accounts Wilde's published short stories, apart from *Lord Arthur Savile's Crime*, are inferior examples of the stories that formed such an integral part of his talks.

It is as a playwright that Oscar Wilde achieved the most fame, and his plays reveal a generous supply of examples of his spontaneous conversation. His three early comedies abound with his wit and epigrams, and the concise, exact, well-turned sentences snapping like snuff-boxes, re-create the atmosphere and very air that Wilde breathed.

He regarded his plays as the most important things he had done, and certainly they supply the best, if fragmentary, record of his gassamer talk. The plots are slight, and mainly serve as thin thread holding together the large collection of gay, brightly coloured decorations that are his epigrams and conversational sallies.

The wittiest characters in his plays are Wilde himself in many guises, whilst the ancillary beings who share or prompt the sayings are merely the back-cloth, sketched in to serve as a setting for his own vivid personality.

Many of the sayings carry a ring of familiarity and indeed many of them appear in *Dorian Gray*, for Wilde had no compunction in transplanting them from one work to another and those that appealed to him he used time and time again, and always he preserved the sparkle.

In fairness to Wilde in considering his early plays it is as well to take into account the tragi-comic nature of his audiences. Wilde had a greedy desire for public applause and was quite happy to supply the fare to satisfy the public appetite. The Theatre appealed to him as a means of " talking " to thousands at the same time and he was able to sit back and revel in the immediate applause of his listeners. His early plays were written to suit the smiles and tears of his audience. *The Importance of Being Earnest* was written to please himself and it is immeasurably superior to the others. In *Earnest* he clearly reveals the joyous exuberance of his personality; a characteristic which it is impossible to capture in words in describing his talk.

Wilde threw overboard the style of his previous plays when he wrote *Salomé,* and this play reveals an entirely different aspect of his nature. He wrote it in French and it was translated into English by Lord Alfred Douglas, and it probably bears the distinction of being the only important play written in French by an English (or Irish) dramatist. It is mainly in the form of short, staccato sentences, and Wilde shows the same delight in lavish and exotic effect; but more than anything else Wilde demonstrates his wonderful sense of drama. *Salomé* has an eerie atmosphere of impending doom and we are allowed to peer into that strange world of unreality into which his mind often wandered.

Whilst in Reading Gaol Wilde planned two plays similar to *Salomé.* They were to be entitled *Ahab and Isabel* and *Pharaoh,* but although he talked about them, and even quoted from them, the plays were never written.

Wilde's plays do not pay full tribute to his brilliant intellect and we must look elsewhere for illustrations of his learning and breadth of thought.

From the early days of his lectures in America, Wilde delighted in appearing erudite, and in one lecture alone, for example, he appeals to Goethe, Rousseau, Scott, Coleridge, Wordsworth, Blake, Homer, Dante, Morris, Keats, Chaucer, Hunt, Millais, Rossetti, Burne-Jones, Ruskin, Swinburne, Tennyson, Plato, Aristotle, Leonardo da Vinci, Edgar Allan Poe, Phidias, Michelangelo, Sophocles, Milton, Fra Angelico, Rubens, Leopardi, Titian, Georgione, Hugo, Balzac, Shakespeare, Mazzini and Petrarch, Baudelaire, Theocritus, and Gautier, but this " pose " as a scholar was a true one.

In *Intentions* (which includes *The Critic as Artist; The Decay of Lying; Pen, Pencil and Poison;* and *The Truth of Masks*) he reveals his attitude of mind and his adventurous, questing thoughts, and this work is a perfect example of his intellectual conversation.

The talk is in the form of dialogues, in which Wilde poses the questions and supplies the answers. In this way he exhibits every aspect of his subject and ventilates his theories on art and life and thought. The dialogues are perfect in construction and even appear too exact to have been included in actual talk. But

27

this was Wilde's manner of speaking, and if, by its excellence it appears unreal it has captured the very spirit of his serious conversation. Indeed, one is apt to be blinded by Wilde's dazzling imagery of words to the meticulous construction of his paragraphs and the thoughtful care he used in assembling his arguments. Undoubtedly, *Intentions* stands alone of its kind as an expression of the attitude of mind and subtle reasoning of a brilliant intellectual.

The Soul of Man Under Socialism is Wilde's airy venture into social reform and in its flippant detachment from practical policy it reveals the artificiality of his attitude to Life.

It is said that he attended a meeting at which Shaw expounded his doctrine of Fabian Socialism (Wilde, always unable to resist an opportunity of speaking in public, also spoke) and that straightaway he went home and wrote his essay. The result, however, bears no relationship to Shaw's dogma, and Wilde preached Socialism as a method of attaining Individualism.

It is possible that Wilde was influenced to some degree by Edward Bellamy's novel of idealistic socialism " Looking Backward ", which at that time had sold more than a million copies, for in the same way Wilde advocates the abolition of property and the free choice of occupation to allow the individual to develope his personality. Wilde sides with the hypothetical social reform that removes the anxiety of maintaining existence and relegates work to a pastime. His main use for Socialism is that it should assist Art. As propaganda for social reform *The Soul of Man Under Socialism* is relatively unimportant but as conversation centred upon the position of Art in relation to Life it is delightful and stimulating.

In his essay Wilde shows sympathy with the poor but his method of helping them is to entertain them, and he does not suggest means of improving their position. Until society sent him to prison his evaluation of society was based upon London Society. In prison, for perhaps the first time in his life, he was really face to face with sordid reality and in his two letters to the *Daily Chronicle* he shows a deeper and more genuine understanding of the poor and the unfortunate.

His heart-cry of indignation at the treatment meted out to

children was fifty years ahead of the period, for it is couched in the language and sentiments of to-day, and his two letters urging prison reform reveal his deep and genuine feelings of sympathy. But it was only by sharing their tribulations that he was able to appreciate fully their wretchedness.

In examining Wilde's works mention must be made of *De Profundis* and *The Ballad of Reading Gaol,* the two monuments to his tragedy.

The character of Wilde's prose in *De Profundis* is similar to many of the paragraphs of *Intentions,* and it is a remarkable and unusual work, more serious than anything else he wrote with the exception of *Reading Gaol.*

The original manuscript is in the form of eighty close-written sheets of prison notepaper, and is a letter to Lord Alfred Douglas which Wilde wrote in Reading Gaol. He was only supplied with one sheet of notepaper at a time; when he had filled a sheet it was taken away and he did not see it again. Despite this handicap of not being able to peruse and correct his writings, Wilde perfectly maintained the flow of his thoughts. It is amazing that even in his state of mental torment he was able to call upon that clarity of mind and fluent use of language which were such salient features of his discourses. In his own words he recounts the steps of his downfall and tells of his fatal friendship with Lord Alfred Douglas.

At first, Wilde suffered the brooding melancholy of a desperately unhappy introvert and *De Profundis* is a magnificently eloquent but self-pitying document, revealing new and hitherto unsuspected depths to his emotional outlook. Later, even amidst his ruin, he was able to view his downfall objectively as an experience of acute misery.

In Reading Gaol he suffered all the indignities of prison routine, but without doubt the rule which caused him the greatest misery was the one of silence. Every day the prisoners walked for one hour in a long circle round the prison-yard, under the watchful eyes of the warders. In this exercise period the prisoners whispered to each other without moving their lips, and this constituted their only oral communication.

For six long weeks Wilde endured silence and then, one day

he heard a voice behind him, say : " Oscar Wilde, I am sorry for you. It must be worse for you than for us." Wilde almost fainted, and whispered back : " No; it's the same for all of us." Thus, he met his fellow-prisoners, and afterwards he wrote : " The only humanizing influence in prison is the prisoners."

The Ballad of Reading Gaol, which is one of Wilde's greatest works, is magnificent as poetry, and stirring as propaganda against the then terrible conditions of prison life. It is a strong proof of the change of mind and attitude to life which took place whilst he was in prison. The human, sympathetic element which always lurked behind his words is articulate on its own account and speaks in a loud voice for the good of humanity.

With fitting irony Oscar Wilde's epitaph on his tomb at Père-Lachaise, Paris, consists of the following lines from *Reading Gaol:*

> And alien tears will fill for him
> Pity's long-broken urn,
> For his mourners will be outcast men,
> And outcasts always mourn.

The tomb, the work of Epstein, was put up in 1912 by, it is said, an Englishwoman who wished to remain anonymous.

With his writings Oscar Wilde has defeated the anonymity of Death, but, regrettably, they are only brief excerpts that he chose to leave as a record from his far richer conversation.

George Bernard Shaw wrote of Oscar Wilde : " He was incomparably the greatest talker of his time—perhaps of all time " —a fitting tribute from one Irishman of genius to another.

I

MEN

Oscar Wilde lived in an age of fainting femininity and masculine muscularity. Men exerted the dominance of their sex and relegated women to a position of quiescent inactivity and idealistic purity.

In this period, Shaw the Socialist, was a prominent figure of Fabianism and social reform, whilst Wilde the Hedonist, led the revolt against middle-class equanimity and Victorian respectability. Oscar Wilde, with his preoccupation with beauty and aestheticism, was the direct opposite of the current ideal of Victorian manhood; yet he, who was so unlike the period, has come to represent it.

*

Men become old, but they never become good.

Lady Windermere's Fan.

*

MRS. ALLONBY : I delight in men over seventy, they always offer one the devotion of a lifetime.   *A Woman of No Importance.*

*

I sometimes think that God in creating man, somewhat overestimated His ability.   *In Conversation.*

*

How many men there are in modern life who would like to see their past burning to white ashes before them?

An Ideal Husband.

*

Bachelors are not fashionable any more. They are a damaged lot. Too much is known about them.   *An Ideal Husband.*

Formerly we used to canonize our heroes. The modern method is to vulgarize them. Cheap editions of great books may be delightful, but cheap editions of great men are absolutely detestable.   *The Critic as Artist.*

*

No man is rich enough to buy back his past.
                                             An Ideal Husband.

*

MRS. ALLONBY: Man, poor, awkward, reliable, necessary man belongs to a sex that has been rational for millions and millions of years. He can't help himself. It is in his race. The History of Woman is very different. We have always been picturesque protests against the mere existence of common sense. We saw its dangers from the first.   *A Woman of No Importance.*

*

The evolution of man is slow. The injustice of man is great.
                              The Soul of Man Under Socialism.

*

. . . one is tempted to define man as a rational animal who always loses his temper when he is called upon to act in accordance with the dictates of his reason.   *The Critic as Artist.*

*

A man who moralizes is usually a hypocrite, and a woman who moralizes is invariably plain.   *Lady Windermere's Fan.*

*

He must be quite respectable. One has never heard his name before in the whole course of one's life, which speaks volumes for a man, nowadays.   *A Woman of No Importance.*

*

By persistently remaining single, a man converts himself into a permanent public temptation. Men should be more careful; this very celibacy leads weaker vessels astray.
                              The Importance of Being Earnest.

CECILY: A man who is much talked about is always attractive. One feels there must be something in him, after all.

The Importance of Being Earnest.

＊

Rich bachelors should be heavily taxed. It is not fair that some men should be happier than others. *In Conversation.*

＊

Men are horribly tedious when they are good husbands, and abominably conceited when they are not.

A Woman of No Importance.

＊

A man cannot always be estimated by what he does. He may keep the law, and yet be worthless. He may break the law and yet be fine. *The Soul of Man Under Socialism.*

＊

When a man acts he is a puppet. When he describes he is a poet. *In Conversation.*

＊

LADY WINDERMERE: . . . I don't like compliments, and I don't see why a man should think he is pleasing a woman enormously when he says to her a whole heap of things that he doesn't mean.

Lady Windermere's Fan.

＊

He has one of those terribly weak natures that are not susceptible to influence. *An Ideal Husband.*

＊

On a view from an hotel window:
Oh, that is altogether immaterial, except to the proprietor, who of course charges it in the bill. A gentleman never looks out of the window. *In Conversation.*

33

A bad man is the sort of man who admires innocence, and a bad woman is the sort of woman a man never gets tired of.
A Woman of No Importance.

*

If a man is a gentleman, he knows quite enough, and if he is not a gentleman, whatever he knows is bad for him.
The Picture of Dorian Gray.

*

The husbands of very beautiful women belong to the criminal classes. *The Picture of Dorian Gray.*

*

MRS. ALLONBY : The Ideal Man . ... he should always say much more than he means, and always mean much more than he says.
A Woman of No Importance.

*

What on earth should we men do going about with purity and innocence? A carefully thought-out buttonhole is much more effective. *Lady Windermere's Fan.*

*

MRS. ALLONBY : The Ideal Man . . . should never run down other pretty women. That would show he had no taste or make one suspect that he had too much.
A Woman of No Importance.

*

When a man is old enough to do wrong he should be old enough to do right also. *A Woman of No Importance.*

*

What a man really has, is what is in him. What is outside of him should be a matter of no importance.
The Soul of Man Under Socialism.

. . . one of Nature's gentlemen, the worst type of gentleman I know. *Lady Windermere's Fan.*

*

Men who are trying to do something for the world, are always insufferable, when the world has done something for *them,* they are charming. *In Conversation.*

*

MRS. ALLONBY: He should invariably praise us for whatever qualities he knows we haven't got. But he should be pitiless, quite pitiless, in reproaching us for the virtues we have never dreamed of possessing. *A Woman of No Importance.*

*

MRS. ALLONBY: Nothing is so aggravating as calmness. There is something positively brutal about the good temper of most modern men. I wonder we women stand it as well as we do. *A Woman of No Importance.*

*

When men give up saying what is charming, they give up thinking what is charming. *Lady Windermere's Fan.*

*

Man can believe the impossible, but man can never believe the improbable. *The Decay of Lying.*

*

The true perfection of man lies, not in what man has, but in what man is. *The Soul of Man Under Socialism.*

II

WOMEN

Men are appealed to through their eyes—women through their ears. It was inevitable, therefore, that women should find Oscar Wilde attractive. They were charmed by his conversation, his understanding, his flattery, his sympathy and his apparent interest in them.

On his return from America Wilde, talking of the fuss made of him by the American women, said he had employed two secretaries, one being responsible for the autographs, the other for the locks of his hair, and that in six months the first had died of writer's cramp—the other was completely bald.

*

One should never trust a woman who tells one her real age. A woman who would tell one that, would tell one anything.

A Woman of No Importance.

*

Women—Sphinxes without secrets.

A Woman of No Importance.

*

Crying is the refuge of plain women but the ruin of pretty ones.   *Lady Windermere's Fan.*

*

Women know life too late. That is the difference between men and women.   *A Woman of no Importance.*

*

Women are meant to be loved, not to be understood.

The Sphinx Without a Secret.

36

It takes a thoroughly good woman to do a thoroughly stupid thing.   *Lady Windermere's Fan.*

*

Never trust a woman who wears mauve, whatever her age may be, or a woman over thirty-five who is fond of pink ribbons. It always means they have a history.
                                              The Picture of Dorian Gray.

*

I don't know that women are always rewarded for being charming. I think they are usually punished for it!
                                              An Ideal Husband.

*

If a woman really repents, she never wishes to return to the society that has made or seen her ruin.
                                              Lady Windermere's Fan.

*

I don't think there is a woman in the world who would not be a little flattered if one made love to her. It is that which makes women so irresistibly adorable.   *A Woman of No Importance.*

*

Good women have such limited views of life, their horizon is so small, their interests are so petty.   *A Woman of No Importance.*

*

She'll never love you unless you are always at her heels; women like to be bothered.   *Vera, or The Nihilists.*

*

A woman will flirt with anybody in the world as long as other people are looking on.   *The Picture of Dorian Gray.*

Plain women are always jealous of their husbands. Beautiful women never have time. They are always so occupied in being jealous of other people's husbands.

A Woman of No Importance.

*

Thirty-five is a very attractive age, London society is full of women of the very highest birth who have, of their own free choice, remained thirty-five for years.

The Importance of Being Earnest.

*

It is perfectly brutal the way most women nowadays behave to men who are not their husbands.   *Lady Windermere's Fan.*

*

Women forgive adoration; that is quite as much as should be expected from them.   *A Woman of No Importance.*

*

Mrs. Allonby : We women adore failures. They lean on us.

A Woman of No Importance.

*

Women defend themselves by attacking, just as they attack by sudden and strange surrender.   *The Picture of Dorian Gray.*

*

No woman, plain or pretty, has any common sense at all. Common sense is the privilege of our sex.   *An Ideal Husband.*

*

Women are a decorative sex. They never have anything to say, but they say it charmingly. Women represent the triumph of matter over mind, just as men represent the triumph of mind over morals.   *The Picture of Dorian Gray.*

38

I don't mind plain women being Puritans. It is the only excuse they have for being plain.

A Woman of No Importance.

*

Women love us for our defects. If we have enough of them, they will forgive us everything, even our own gigantic intellects.

A Woman of No Importance.

*

My dear young lady, there was a great deal of truth, I dare say, in what you said, and you looked very pretty while you said it, which is much more important.

A Woman of No Importance.

*

I don't believe in women thinking too much. Women should think in moderation, as they should do all things in moderation.

A Woman of No Importance.

*

American girls are as clever at concealing their parents as English women are at concealing their past.

The Picture of Dorian Gray.

*

Women have no appreciation of good looks; at least good women have not.   *The Picture of Dorian Gray.*

*

How hard good women are!
How weak bad men are!   *Lady Windermere's Fan.*

*

No woman should have a memory. Memory in a woman is the beginning of dowdiness.   *A Woman of No Importance.*

The three women I have most admired are Queen Victoria, Sarah Bernhardt and Lily Langtry. I would have married any one of them with pleasure. The first had great dignity, the second a lovely voice, the third a perfect figure. *In Conversation.*

*

The one charm of the past is that it is past. But women never know when the curtain has fallen.
The Picture of Dorian Gray.

*

I am afraid that women appreciate cruelty, downright cruelty, more than anything else. They have wonderfully primitive instincts. We have emancipated them, but they remain slaves looking for their masters all the same.
The Picture of Dorian Gray.

*

Every woman is a rebel, and usually in wild revolt against herself. *A Woman of No Importance.*

*

Every woman does talk too much. *Vera, or The Nihilists.*

*

The English young lady is the dragon of good taste.
An Ideal Husband.

*

What have women who have not sinned to do with me, or I with them? We do not understand each other.
A Woman of No Importance.

*

Women are not meant to judge us, but to forgive us when we need forgiveness Pardon not punishment, is their mission.
An Ideal Husband.

Most women in London, nowadays, seem to furnish their rooms with nothing but orchids, foreigners, and French novels.

A Woman of No Importance.

*

She looks like a woman with a past. Most pretty women do.

An Ideal Husband.

*

Women are the most reliable as they have no memory for the important.

Letter to Robert Ross written from Reading Prison.

*

Women have a wonderful instinct about things. They can discover everything except the obvious. *An Ideal Husband.*

*

GERALD : . . . there are many different kinds of women, aren't there?
LORD ILLINGWORTH : Only two kinds in society : the plain and the coloured.
GERALD : But there are good women in society, aren't there?
LORD ILLINGWORTH : Far too many.

A Woman of No Importance.

*

The history of women is the history of the worst form of tyranny the world has ever known. The tyranny of the weak over the strong. It is the only tyranny that lasts.

A Woman of No Importance.

*

Women give to men the very gold of their lives. But they invariably want it back in small change. *In Conversation.*

*

More women grow old nowadays through the faithfulness of their admirers than through anything else.

An Ideal Husband.

Immoral women are rarely attractive. What made her quite irresistible was that she was unmoral. *In Conversation.*

*

LORD ILLINGWORTH: . . . What a typical woman you are! You talk sentimentally, and you are thoroughly selfish the whole time. *A Woman of No Importance.*

*

It is said, of course, that she ran away twice before she was married. But you know how unfair people often are. I myself don't believe she ran away more than once.
A Woman of No Importance.

*

I have met hundreds of good women. I never seem to meet any but good women. The world is perfectly packed with good women. To know them is a middle-class education.
Lady Windermere's Fan.

*

Women, as some witty Frenchman once put it, inspire us with the desire to do masterpieces, and always prevent us from carrying them out. *The Picture of Dorian Gray.*

*

She was made to be an ambassador's wife. She certainly has a wonderful faculty of remembering people's names, and forgetting their faces. *A Woman of No Importance.*

*

I am sick of women who love me. Women who hate me are much more interesting. *The Picture of Dorian Gray.*

*

No man has any real success in this world unless he has got women to back him, and women rule society. *In Conversation.*

There is one thing infinitely more pathetic than to have lost the woman one is in love with, and that is to have won her and found out how shallow she is.   *In Conversation.*

*

The only way to behave to a woman is to make love to her, if she is pretty, and to some one else, if she is plain.
                              The Importance of Being Earnest.

*

GERALD : It is very difficult to understand women, is it not?
LORD ILLINGWORTH : You should never try to understand them. Women are pictures.   Men are problems.
                              A Woman of No Importance.

*

I don't think now that people can be divided into the good and the bad as though they were two separate races or creatures. What are called good women may have terrible things in them, mad moods of recklessness, assertion, jealousy, sin. Bad women, as they are termed, may have in them sorrow, repentance, pity, sacrifice.   *Lady Windermere's Fan.*

*

The most important consolation that women find in modern life is taking someone else's admirer when one loses one's own. In good society that always whitewashes a woman.
                              The Picture of Dorian Gray.

*

MRS. CHEVELEY : The strength of women comes from the fact that psychology cannot explain us.   Men can be analysed and women . . . merely adored.   *An Ideal Husband.*

*

Repentance is quite out of date and besides, if a woman really repents, she has to go to a bad dressmaker, otherwise no one believes her.   *Lady Windermere's Fan.*

Being adored is a nuisance. Women treat us just as Humanity treats its Gods. They worship us and are always asking us to do something for them.   *The Picture of Dorian Gray.*

*

She is a peacock in everything but beauty.
                                      The Picture of Dorian Gray.

*

Women are never disarmed by compliments. Men always are. That is the difference between the sexes.
                                              An Ideal Husband.

*

That awful memory of woman! What a fearful thing it is! And what an utter intellectual stagnation it reveals! One should absorb the colour of life, but one should never remember its details. Details are always vulgar.
                                      The Picture of Dorian Gray.

*

I think there are many things women should never forgive.
                                      A Woman of No Importance.

*

The only way a woman can ever reform a man is by boring him so completely that he loses all possible interest in life.
                                      The Picture of Dorian Gray.

*

If a woman can't make her mistakes charming, she is only a female.   *Lord Arthur Savile's Crime.*

*

It is only very ugly or very beautiful women who ever hide their faces.   *The Duchess of Padua.*

*

As long as a woman can look ten years younger than her own daughter, she is perfectly satisfied.
                                      The Picture of Dorian Gray.

Women are wonderfully practical, much more practical than we are. In situations of that kind we often forget to say anything about marriage and they always remind us.

The Picture of Dorian Gray.

*

Wicked women bother one. Good women bore one. That is the only difference between them. *Lady Windermere's Fan.*

*

A poor woman who is not straight is a prostitute, but a rich one is a lady of fashion. *In Conversation.*

*

Women are always on the side of morality, public and private. *A Woman of No Importance.*

*

A chase after a beautiful woman is always exciting.

Vera, or The Nihilists.

*

In the case of very fascinating women, sex is a challenge, not a defence. *An Ideal Husband.*

*

There is only one real tragedy in a woman's life. The fact that her past is always her lover, and her future invariably her husband. *An Ideal Husband.*

*

A woman whose size in gloves is seven and three-quarters never knows much about anything. *An Ideal Husband.*

*

I prefer women with a past. They're always so demned amusing to talk to. *Lady Windermere's Fan.*

The plain women are very useful. If you want to gain a reputation for respectability, you have merely to take them down to supper. The other women are very charming. They commit one mistake, however. They paint in order to try and look young. Our grandmothers painted in order to try and talk brilliantly. *The Picture of Dorian Gray.*

*

MISS PRISM : A misanthrope I can understand—a womanthrope, never! *The Importance of Being Earnest.*

III

PEOPLE

The people of Wilde's day lived in an age of carefree optimism, turning a complacent face away from the poverty and disturbing working conditions of the period. Decorous gaiety and rosy romanticism took the place of realism.

This public only admired a person whose personality they believed they understood. Wilde's nature was too complex to allow him to be popular with the masses, and the audiences who applauded his plays were even more vociferous in condemning his conduct. Even at the height of his success Wilde was an object of derision.

He wrote in the idiom of the nineties, and his wit, epigrams, and paradoxes, were perfectly in tune with the voice of the period; he was successful, but disliked.

Once whilst walking down Piccadilly with an acquaintance he heard a passer-by say, "There goes that bloody fool Oscar Wilde!" Wilde turned to his companion and with perfect composure remarked, "It's extraordinary how soon one gets known in London."

*

People who count their chickens before they are hatched, act very wisely, because chickens run about so absurdly that it is impossible to count them accurately.

Letter from Paris May 1900.

*

One can always be kind to people about whom one cares nothing. *The Picture of Dorian Gray.*

*

It is absurd to divide people into good and bad. People are either charming or tedious. *Lady Windermere's Fan.*

47

People who want to say merely what is sensible should say it to themselves before they come down to breakfast in the morning, never after. *In Conversation.*

*

When people talk to us about others they are usually dull. When they talk to us about themselves they are nearly always interesting. *The Critic as Artist.*

*

You ask me what is my feeling towards my audiences—towards the public. Which public? There are as many publics as there are personalities . . . I am not nervous on the night that I am producing a new play. I am exquisitely indifferent. My nervousness ends at the last dress rehearsal. I know then what effect my play, as presented upon the stage, has produced upon me. My interest in the play ends there, and I feel curiously envious of the public—they have such wonderfully fresh emotions in store for them . . . It is the public, not the play, that I desire to make a success . . . The public makes a success when it realizes that a play is a work of art. On the three first nights I have had in London the public has been most successful, and, had the dimensions of the stage admitted of it, I would have called them before the curtain . . . The artist is always the munificent patron of the public.

I am very fond of the public, and, personally, I always patron-ize the public very much. *In an Interview.*

*

As a rule, people who act lead the most commonplace lives. They are good husbands or faithful wives, or something tedious. *The Picture of Dorian Gray.*

*

The more one analyses people, the more all reasons for analysis disappear. Sooner or later one comes to that dreadful universal thing called human nature. *The Decay of Lying.*

The one thing that the public dislike is novelty. Any attempt to extend the subject matter of art is extremely distasteful to the public. *The Soul of Man Under Socialism.*

*

Whenever people talk to me about the weather, I always feel certain that they mean something else.
The Importance of Being Earnest.

*

There are only two kinds of people who are really fascinating —people who know absolutely everything and people who know absolutely nothing. *The Picture of Dorian Gray.*

*

The public have an insatiable curiosity to know everything, except what is worth knowing.
The Soul of Man Under Socialism.

*

Philanthropic people lose all sense of humanity. It is their distinguishing characteristic. *The Picture of Dorian Gray.*

*

Most men and women are forced to perform parts for which they have no qualifications. *Lord Arthur Savile's Crime.*

*

The private lives of men and women should not be told to the public. The public have nothing to do with them at all.
The Soul of Man Under Socialism.

*

It is perfectly monstrous the way people go about, nowadays, saying things against one behind one's back that are absolutely and entirely true. *A Woman of No Importance.*

*

Nowadays people know the price of everything and the value of nothing. *The Picture of Dorian Gray.*

Well bred people always stay in exactly the same place as we
do.   *The Birthday of the Infanta.*

*

I'm sure I don't know half the people who come to my house.
Indeed, from all I hear, I shouldn't like to.   *An Ideal Husband.*

*

Everyone is born a king, and most people die in exile, like
most kings.   *A Woman of No Importance.*

*

People are either hunting for husbands, or hiding from them.
                                                An Ideal Husband.

*

You can't go anywhere without meeting clever people.   The
thing has become an absolute public nuisance.   I wish to goodness we had a few fools left.
                                    The Importance of Being Earnest.

*

I like men who have a future and women who have a past.
                                                The Picture of Dorian Gray.

*

. . . as for the People, what of them and their authority?
. . . Their authority is a thing blind, deaf, hideous, grotesque,
tragic, amusing, serious, and obscene.   It is impossible for the
artist to live with the People.   All despots bribe.   The People
bribe and brutalize.   Who told them to exercise authority?   They
were made to live, to listen, and to love.   Someone has done
them a great wrong.   They have taken the sceptre of the Prince.
How should they use it?   They have taken the triple tiara of
the Pope.   How should they carry its burden?   They are as a
clown whose heart is broken.   They are as a priest whose soul
is not yet born.   Let all who love Beauty pity them.
   Though they themselves love not Beauty, yet let them pity
themselves.   Who taught them the trick of tyranny?
                                    The Soul of Man Under Socialism.

50

London is too full of fogs—and serious people. Whether the fogs produce the serious people or whether, the serious people produce the fogs, I don't know, but the whole thing rather gets on my nerves.   *Lady Windermere's Fan.*

*

Nowadays most people die of a sort of creeping common sense, and discover when it is too late that the only things one never regrets are one's mistake.

The Picture of Dorian Gray.

*

I like persons better than principles and I like persons with no principles better than anything else in the world.

The Picture of Dorian Gray.

*

I never approve, or disapprove, of anything now. It is an absurd attitude to take towards life. We are not sent into the world to air our moral Prejudices. I never take any notice of what common people say, and I never interfere with what charming people do.   *The Picture of Dorian Gray.*

*

LORD HENRY: I like to find out people for myself. But Lady Brandon treats her guests exactly as an auctioneer treats his goods. She either explains them entirely away, or tells one everything about them except what one wants to know.

The Picture of Dorian Gray.

*

The only real people are the people who never existed and if a novelist is base enough to go to life for his personages he should at least pretend that they are creations and not boast of them as copies.   *The Decay of Lying.*

IV

ART

To Wilde Art was more real than life and he insisted that nature imitated art. This belief is perfectly exemplified in "Intentions," and in fact, is evident in all his works. He still maintained his theories when ultimately he was face-to-face with sordid reality. Throughout America he lectured on "The English Renaissance of Art," "House Decoration," and "Art and the Handicrafts man." No doubt he earnestly believed that the aesthetic movement was the purpose of his existence, and in one of his lectures told "how it first came to me at all to create an artistic movement in England."

Whistler said of Wilde—"What has Oscar in common with Art except that he dines at our tables and picks from our platters the plums for the pudding that he peddles in the provinces? Oscar—the amiable, irresponsible, esurient Oscar—with no more sense of a picture than he has of the fit of a coat—has the courage of opinions of others!"

Imperturbably Oscar replied, "with our James vulgarity begins at home and should be allowed to stay there," and quite indifferent to the caustic wit of Whistler used the phrase, "the courage of the opinions of others" in "The Decay of Lying."

*

It is only an auctioneer who can equally and impartially admire all schools of Art.   *The Critic as Artist.*

*

All art is immoral. For emotion for the sake of emotion is the aim of art, and emotion for the sake of action is the aim of life.
                                        The Critic as Artist.

*

The best that one can say of most modern creative art is that it is just a little less vulgar than reality.   *The Critic as Artist.*

An age that has no criticism is either an age in which art is immobile, hieratic, and confined to the reproduction of formal types, or an age that possesses no art at all.

The Critic as Artist.

*

We are over-run by a set of people who, when poet or painter passes away, arrive at the house along with the undertaker, and forget that their one duty is to behave as mutes.

The Critic as Artist.

*

Art is the most intense mode of Individualism that the world has known.   *The Soul of man under Socialism.*

*

Varnishing is the only artistic process with which the Royal Academicians are thoroughly familiar.   *In Conversation.*

*

We can forgive a man for making a useful thing as long as he does not admire it. The only excuse for making a useless thing is that one admires it intensely.

All art is quite useless.   *The Picture of Dorian Gray.*

*

We live in an age when men treat art as if it were meant to be a form of autobiography.   *The Picture of Dorian Gray.*

*

Mediocrity weighing mediocrity in the balance, and incompetence applauding its brother—that is the spectacle which the artistic activity of England affords us from time to time.

The Critic as Artist.

*

Modern pictures are, no doubt, delightful to look at. At least, some of them are. But they are quite impossible to live with; they are too clever, too assertive, too intellectual. Their meaning is too obvious, and their method too clearly defined. One exhausts what they have to say in a very short time, and then they become as tedious as one's relations.   *The Critic as Artist.*

The facts of art are divine, but the essence of artistic effect is unity.   *The Truth of Masks.*

*

The true artist is a man who believes absolutely in himself, because he is absolutely himself.
                                The Soul of Man Under Socialism.

*

ERNEST: Simply this: that in the best days of art there were no art-critics.
GILBERT: I seem to have heard that observation before, Ernest. It has all the vitality of error and all the tediousness of an old friend.   *The Critic as Artist.*

*

I am very fond of the work of some of the impressionist painters of Paris and London. For a class that welcomes the incompetent with sympathetic eagerness, and that confuses the bizarre with the beautiful, and vulgarity with truth, they are extremely accomplished. They can do etchings that have the brilliancy of epigrams, pastels that are as fascinating as paradoxes, and as for their portraits, whatever the commonplace may say against them, no one can deny that they possess that unique and wonderful charm which belongs to pure fiction.
                                            The Critic as Artist.

*

Bad artists always admire each other's work. They call it being large-minded and free from prejudice. But a truly great artist cannot conceive of life being shown, or beauty fashioned, under any conditions other than those he has selected.
                                            The Critic as Artist.

*

Most of our modern portrait painters are doomed to oblivion. They never paint what they see. They paint what the public sees, and the public never sees anything.   *The Decay of Lying.*

Things are because we see them, and what we see, and how we see it depends on the Arts that have influenced us. At present, people see fogs, not because there are fogs, but because poets and painters have taught them the mysterious loveliness of such effects. There may have been fogs for centuries in London. I dare say there were. But no one saw them, and so we do not know anything about them. They did not exist till Art had invented them. Now, it must be admitted, fogs are carried to excess. They have become the mere mannerism of a clique, and the exaggerated realism of their method gives dull people bronchitis. Where the cultured catch an effect, the uncultured catch cold.   *The Decay of Lying.*

*

The Academy is too large and too vulgar. Whenever I have gone there, there have been either so many people that I have not been able to see the pictures, which was dreadful or so many pictures that I have not been able to see the people, which was worse.   *The Picture of Dorian Gray.*

*

Paradox though it may seem—and paradoxes are always dangerous things—it is none the less true that life imitates art far more than art imitates life.   *The Decay of Lying.*

*

The public imagine that, because they are interested in their immediate surroundings, art should be interested in them also, and should take them as her subject matter. But the mere fact that they are interested in these things makes them unsuitable subjects for art.   *The Decay of Lying.*

*

No great artist ever sees things as they really are. If he did he would cease to be an artist.   *The Decay of Lying.*

*

She is like most artists; she is all style without any sincerity.
                                    The Nightingale and the Rose.

55

Nature is elbowing her way into the charmed circle of art.

In Conversation.

*

Nobody of any real culture ever talks about the beauty of a sunset. Sunsets are quite old-fashioned. They belong to the time when Turner was the last note in art. To admire them is a distinct sign of provincialism. Upon the other hand they go on. Yesterday evening Mrs. Arundel insisted on my going to the window and looking at the glorious sky, as she called it. Of course I had to look at it. She is one of those absurdly pretty Philistines, to whom one can deny nothing. And what was it? It was simply a very second-rate Turner, a Turner of bad period, with all the painter's worst faults exaggerated and over-emphasized.

The Decay of Lying.

*

In art, the public accept what has been, because they cannot alter it, not because they can appreciate it.

The Soul of Man Under Socialism.

*

. . . Art's first appeal is neither to the intellect nor to the emotions, but purely to the artistic temperament.

Pen, Pencil and Poison.

*

. . . there are two worlds—the one exists and is never talked about; it is called the real world because there is no need to talk about it in order to see it. The other is the world of Art; one must talk about that, because otherwise it would not exist.

In Conversation.

*

Mr. Quiller is entirely free from affectation of any kind. He rollicks through art with the recklessness of the tourist and describes its beauties with the enthusiasm of the auctioneer. To many, no doubt, he will seem to be somewhat blatant and bumptious, but we prefer to regard him as being simply British.

Review in Pall Mall Gazette.

On Max Beerbohm:
. . . the Gods bestowed on Max the gift of perpetual old age.
In Conversation.

*

No artist has ethical sympathies. An ethical sympathy in an
artist is an unpardonable mannerism of style.
The Picture of Dorian Gray.

*

On Whistler:
Jimmy explains things in the newspapers. Art should always
remain mysterious. Artists, like Gods, must never leave their
pedestals.   *In Conversation.*

*

The only artists I have ever known, who are personally delightful, are bad artists, good artists exist simply in what they make
and consequently are perfectly uninteresting in what they are.
The Picture of Dorian Gray.

*

We try to improve the conditions of the race by means of good
air, free sunlight, wholesome water, and hideous bare buildings
for the better housing of the lower orders. But these things merely
produce health, they do not produce beauty. For this, Art is
required, and the true disciples of the great artist are not his
studio-imitators, but those who become like his work of art, be
they plastic as in Greek days, or pictorial as in modern times; in
a word, Life is Art's best, Art's only pupil.
The Decay of Lying.

*

Art finds her own perfection within, and not outside of, herself.
She is not to be judged by any external standards of resemblance.
She is a veil, rather than a mirror. She has flowers that no
forests know of, birds that no woodland possesses. She makes
and unmakes many worlds, and can draw the moon from heaven
with a scarlet thread. Hers are the forms more real than living
man, and hers the great archetypes of which things that have
existence are but unfinished copies. Nature has, in her eyes, no
law, no uniformity.   *The Decay of Lying.*

. . . the public make use of the classics of a country as a means of checking the progress of Art. They degrade the classics into authorities. They use them as bludgeons for preventing the expression of beauty in new forms. They are always asking a writer why he does not write like somebody else, or a painter why he does not paint like somebody else, quite oblivious of the fact that if either of them did anything of the kind he would cease to be an artist. *The Soul of Man Under Socialism.*

*

There are fashions in art just as there are fashions in dress, and perhaps none of us can quite free ourselves from the influence of custom and the influence of novelty.

Pen, Pencil and Poison.

*

There are two ways of disliking art . . . One is to dislike it. The other is to like it rationally. *The Critic as Artist.*

*

The only portraits in which one believes are portraits where there is very little of the sitter and a very great deal of the artist.

The Decay of Lying.

*

Nature is always behind the age. It takes a great artist to be thoroughly modern. *In Conversation.*

*

In a very ugly and sensible age, the arts borrow, not from life but from each other. *Pen, Pencil and Poison.*

*

Popularity is the crown of laurel which the world puts on bad art. Whatever is popular is wrong.

Lecture to Art Students.

*

Is it really *all* done by hand? *Remark on seeing Frith's vast Painting, " Derby Day."* *In Conversation.*

*

. . . the great superiority of France over England is that in France every bourgeois wants to be an artist, whereas in England every artist wants to be a bourgeois. *In Conversation.*

Most of our elderly English painters spend most of their wicked wasted lives in poaching upon the domain of the poets, marring their motives by clumsy treatment, and striving to render by visible form or colour, the marvel of what is invisible, the splendour of what is not seen. Their pictures are, as a natural consequence, insufferably tedious. They have degraded the invisible arts into the obvious arts and the only thing not worth looking at is the obvious. *The Critic as Artist.*

*

On the staircase stood several Royal Academicians, disguised as artists. *In Conversation.*

*

That poetic school of artists who imagine that the true way of idealising a sitter is to paint someone else. *In Conversation.*

*

The originality which we ask from the artist is originality of treatment, not of subject. It is only the unimaginative who ever invent. The true artist is known by the use he makes of what he annexes, and he annexes everything. *As a Reviewer.*

*

Art never expresses anything but itself. It has an independent life, just as Thought has, and develops purely on its own lines. It is not necessarily realistic in an age of realism, nor spiritual in an age of faith. So far from being the creation of its time, it is usually in direct opposition to it, and the only history it preserves for us is the history of its own progress. Sometimes it returns upon its footsteps, and revives some antique form, as happened in the archaistic movement of late Greek Art, and in the pre-Raphaelite movement of our own day. At other times it entirely anticipates its age, and produces in one century work that it takes another century to understand, to appreciate, and to enjoy. In no case does it reproduce its age. To pass from the art of a time to the time itself is the great mistake that all historians commit.
. . . All bad art comes from returning to Life and Nature, and

elevating them to ideals. Life and Nature may sometimes be used as part of Art's rough material, before they are of any real service to Art they must be translated into artistic conventions. The moment Art surrenders its imaginative medium it surrenders everything. As a method Realism is a complete failure, and the two things that every artist should avoid are modernity of form and modernity of subject matter. To us, who live in the nineteenth century, any century is a suitable subject for art except our own. The only beautiful things are the things that do not concern us. It is . . . exactly because Hecuba is nothing to us that her sorrows are so suitable a motive for tragedy. Besides, it is only the modern that ever becomes old fashioned . . . Life goes faster than Realism, but Romanticism is always in front of Life.

. . . Life imitates Art far more than Art imitates Life. This results not merely from Life's imitative instinct, but from the fact that the self-conscious aim of Life is to find expression, and that Art offers certain beautiful forms through which it may realize that energy. It is a theory that has never been put forward before, but it is extremely fruitful, and throws an entirely new light upon the history of Art.

It follows, as a corollary from this, that external Nature also imitates Art. The only effects she can show us are effects that we have already seen through poetry, or in paintings. This is the secret of Nature's charm, as well as the explanation of Nature's weakness.

. . . Lying, the telling of beautiful untrue things, is the proper aim of Art.   *The Decay of Lying.*

*

No artist desires to prove anything. Even things that are true can be proved.   *The Picture of Dorian Gray.*

*

No spectator of art needs a more perfect mood of receptivity than the spectator of a play. The moment he seeks to exercise authority he becomes the avowed enemy of Art, and of himself. Art does not mind. It is he who suffers.

                              The Soul of Man Under Socialism.

Only mediocrities progress. An artist revolves in a cycle of masterpieces, the first of which is no less perfect than the last.

In a Newspaper Article.

*

That curious mixture of bad painting and good intentions that always entitles a man to be called a representative British artist. *In Conversation.*

*

To fail and to die young is the only hope for a Scotsman who wishes to remain an artist. *In Conversation.*

*

Whistler is indeed one of the very greatest masters of painting in my opinion. And I may add that in this opinion Mr. Whistler himself entirely concurs. *From the Pall Mall Gazette.*

*

One touch of Nature may make the whole world kin, but two touches of Nature will destroy any work of Art.

The Decay of Lying.

*

. . . the more we study Art, the less we care for Nature. What Art really reveals to us is Nature's lack of design, her curious crudities, her extraordinary monotony, her absolutely unfinished condition. Nature has good intentions, of course, but, as Aristotle once said, she cannot carry them out.

The Decay of Lying.

*

The proper school to learn art is not Life but Art.

The Decay of Lying.

*

Philosophy may teach us to bear with equanimity the misfortunes of our neighbours, and science resolve the moral sense into a secretion of sugar, but art is what makes the life of each citizen a sacrament. *A Lecture in America.*

Art is our spirited protest, our gallant attempt to teach Nature her proper place. *The Decay of Lying.*

*

To reveal art and conceal the artist is art's aim. *The Picture of Dorian Gray.*

*

Whistler left America in order to remain an artist, and Mr. Sargent to become one. *In Conversation.*

*

He finds that Literature is an inadequate expression of life. That is quite true : but a work of art is an adequate expression of art—that is its aim. Only that. Life is merely the motif of a pattern. *Letter from Napoule, February 1899.*

*

The Public has always, and in every age, been badly brought up. They are continually asking art to be popular, to please their want of taste, to flatter their absurd vanity, to tell them what they have been told before, to show them what they ought to be tired of seeing, to amuse them when they feel heavy after eating too much, and to distract their thoughts when they are wearied of their own stupidity. Now art should never try to be popular. The public should try to make itself artistic. *The Soul of Man Under Socialism.*

*

It is the spectator, and not life, that art really mirrors. *The Picture of Dorian Gray.*

*

All art is at once surface and symbol. Those who go beneath the surface do so at their peril. Those who read the symbol do so at their peril. *The Picture of Dorian Gray.*

*

The Artist is the creator of beautiful things. *The Picture of Dorian Gray.*

On the afternoon of Easter Day I heard vespers at the Lateran :
music quite lovely : at the close a Bishop in red, with red gloves—
such as Pater talks of in Gaston de la Tour—came out on the
balcony and showed us the relics. He was swarthy, and wore a
yellow mitre. A sinister mediæval man, but superbly Gothic,
just like the Bishop carved on stalls or on portals. And when one
thinks that once people mocked at stained-glass attitudes ! They
are the only attitudes for the clothed. The sight of this Bishop,
whom I watched with fascination, filled me with the sense of the
great realism of Gothic Art. Neither in Greek nor in Gothic Art
is there any pose. Posing was invented by bad portrait-painters,
and the first person who posed was a stockbroker, and he has
gone on ever since.

Letter to Robert Ross from Rome, April 1900.

V

LIFE

In the first volume of his Journal, André Gide recalls a conversation he had with Oscar Wilde in Algiers when, with what to Gide many years afterwards seemed impertinence, he criticized Wilde's plays. Wilde listened intently without protest or impatience to Gide's comments of censure and then, half-apologetically, came his now famous and oft-quoted remark: " I put all my genius into my life; I put only my talent into my works." This remark summed up completely Wilde's essential motif of existence.

He was a life-lover and viewed his life as a means of self-expression. He saw Christ as the supreme artist who created with His life, the perfect work of art and Whose teaching was one of self-development.

Wilde visualized his own life as a work of art, something to be moulded into a beautiful form. He was a dilettante, a spectator of life, and even to the end he was able to stand back and observe the magnitude of his catastrophe.

*

The secret of life is never to have an emotion that is unbecoming.   *A Woman of No Importance.*

*

Life is much too important a thing ever to talk seriously about it.   *Vera, of The Nihilists.*

*

The Book of Life begins with a man and woman in a garden. It ends with Revelations.   *A Woman of No Importance.*

*

One's real life is so often the life that one does not lead.
                              In Conversation.

To live is the rarest thing in the world. Most people exist, that is all. *The Soul of Man Under Socialism.*

*

To become a spectator of one's own life is to escape the suffering of life. *The Picture of Dorian Gray.*

*

I hope you don't think you have exhausted life . . . When a man says that, one knows that life has exhausted him.
A Woman of No Importance.

*

Life . . . is simply a *mauvais quart d'heure* made up of exquisite moments. *A Woman of No Importance.*

*

Life is never fair . . . And perhaps it is a good thing for most of us that it is not. *An Ideal Husband.*

*

Death is not a God. He is only the servant of the gods.
La Sainte Courtisane.

*

You must not find symbols in everything you see. It makes life impossible. *Salomé.*

*

. . . the world has been made by fools that wise men should live in it. *A Woman of No Importance.*

*

Misfortunes one can endure—they come from outside, they are accidents. But to suffer for one's own faults—ah!—there is the sting of life! *Lady Windermere's Fan.*

*

Whatever, in fact, is modern in our life we owe to the Greeks. Whatever is an anachronism is due to medievalism.
The Critic as Artist.

To believe is very dull. To doubt is intensely engrossing. To be on the alert is to live; to be lulled into security is to die.

In Conversation.

*

When one is in town one amuses one's self. When one is in the country one amuses other people.

The Importance of Being Earnest.

*

Town life nourishes and perfects all the more civilized elements in man—Shakespeare wrote nothing but doggerel lampoon before he came to London and never penned a line after he left.

In Conversation.

*

Egotism itself, which is so necessary to a proper sense of human dignity, is entirely the result of an indoor life.

The Decay of Lying.

*

Ambition is the last refuge of the failure.

Phrases and Philosophies for the Use of the Young.

*

People should not mistake the means of civilization for the end. The steam engine and the telephone depend entirely for their value on the use to which they are put.   *In Conversation.*

*

FIRST CITIZEN : What is that word reform? What does it mean?
SECOND CITIZEN : Marry, it means leaving things as they are; I like it not.   *The Duchess of Padua.*

*

Whenever there exists a demand, there is *no* supply. This is the only law that explains the extraordinary contrast between the soul of man and man's surroundings. Civilizations continue because people hate them. A modern city is the exact opposite of what everyone wants. Nineteenth-century dress is the result of our horror of the style. The tall hat will last as long as people dislike it.   *Letter to Robert Ross (May 31st, 1897).*

. . . what man has sought for is, indeed, neither pain nor pleasure, but simply Life. Man has sought to live intensely, fully, perfectly. When he can do so without exercising restraint on others, or suffering it ever, and his activities are all pleasurable to him, he will be saner, healthier, more civilized, more himself. Pleasure is Nature's test, her sign of approval. When a man is happy he is in harmony with himself and his environment. The new Individualism, for whose service Socialism, whether it wills it or not, is working, will be perfect harmony. It will be what the Greeks sought for, but could not, except in Thought, realize completely, because they had slaves, and fed them; it will be what the Renaissance sought for, but could not realize completely except in Art, because they had slaves, and starved them. It will be complete, and through it each man will attain to his perfection. The new Individualism is the new Hellenism.

The Soul of Man Under Socialism.

*

Laughter is the primeval attitude towards life—a mode of approach that survives only in artists and criminals!

In Conversation.

*

Give me the luxuries, and anyone can have the necessaries.

In Conversation.

*

"Comfort," said Mr. Podgers, "and modern improvements, and hot water laid on in every bedroom. Your Grace is quite right. Comfort is the only thing our civilization can give us."

Lord Arthur Savile's Crime.

*

I have no ambition to be a popular hero, to be crowned with laurels one year and pelted with stones the next; I prefer dying peaceably in my own bed.   *Vera, or The Nihilists.*

A map of the world that does not include Utopia is not worth even glancing at, for it leaves out the one country at which Humanity is always landing. And when Humanity lands there, it looks out and seeing a better country, sets sail.

The Soul of Man Under Socialism.

*

What other people call one's past has, no doubt, everything to do with them, but absolutely nothing to do with oneself. The man who regards his past is a man who deserves to have no future to look forward to.   *The Critic as Artist.*

*

It is because Humanity has never known where it was going that it has never been able to find its way.

The Critic as Artist.

*

When we have fully discovered the scientific laws that govern life, we shall realize that one person who has more illusions than the dreamer is the man of action.   *The Critic as Artist.*

*

We live in an age that reads too much to be wise, and thinks too much to be beautiful.   *The Picture of Dorian Gray.*

*

The longer one studies life and literature the more strongly one feels that behind everything that is wonderful stands the individual, and that it is not the moment that makes the man but the man who creates the age.   *The Critic as Artist.*

*

I love acting.   It is so much more real than life.

The Picture of Dorian Gray.

*

Nowadays we have so few mysteries left to us that we cannot afford to part with one of them.   *The Critic as Artist.*

As for omens, there is no such thing as an omen. Destiny does not send us heralds. She is too wise or too cruel for that.
The Picture of Dorian Gray.

*

One should absorb the colour of life, but one should never remember its details. Details are always vulgar.
The Picture of Dorian Gray.

*

. . . when the gods wish to punish us they answer our prayers.
An Ideal Husband.

*

Our business is to realize the world as we see it, not to reform it as we know it. *The Model Millionaire.*

*

To chop wood with any advantage to oneself or profit to others, one should not be able to describe the process—the natural life is the unconscious life . . . If I spent my future life reading Baudelaire in a café, I should be leading a more natural life than if I took to hedgers' work or planted cacao in mud-swamps! *Letter from Reading Gaol, April 6, 1897.*

*

We can have in life but one great experience at best, and the secret of life is to reproduce that experience as often as possible.
The Picture of Dorian Gray.

*

Ethics, like natural selection, make existence possible. Aesthetics, like sexual selection, make life lovely and wonderful, fill it with new forms, and give it progress, and variety and change. *The Critic as Artist.*

*

If a man treats life artistically, his brain is in his heart.
The Picture of Dorian Gray.

There are few things easier than to live badly and to die well.
Vera, or The Nihilists.

*

One can live for years sometimes without living at all, and then all life comes crowding into one single hour.
Vera, or The Nihilists.

*

Much is given to some, and little is given to others. Injustice has parcelled out the world, nor is there equal division of aught save sorrow.
The Star Child.

*

How poor a bargain is the life of man, and in how mean a market are we sold.
A Florentine Tragedy.

*

Each man lived his own life and paid his own price for living it. The only pity was one had to pay so often for a single fault.
The Picture of Dorian Gray.

*

In her dealings with man Destiny never closes her accounts.
The Picture of Dorian Gray.

*

You always find out that one's most glaring fault is one's most important virtue. You have the most comforting views of life.
A Woman of No Importance.

*

Good taste is the excuse I've always given for leading such a bad life.
The Importance of Being Earnest.

*

. . . try as we may we cannot get behind things to the reality. And the terrible reason may be that there is no reality in things apart from their appearances.
In Conversation.

Nothing that actually occurs is of the smallest importance.
Phrases and Philosophies for the Use of the Young.

*

Life is terribly deficient in form. Its catastrophes happen in the wrong way and to the wrong people. There is a grotesque horror about its comedies, and its tragedies seem to culminate in farce. *The Critic as Artist.*

*

The chief thing that makes life a failure from this artistic point of view is the thing that lends life its sordid security, the fact that one can never repeat exactly the same emotion.
The Critic as Artist.

*

It is only the gods who taste death. Apollo has passed away, but Hyacinth, whom men say he slew, lives on. Nero and Narcissus are always with us.
Phrases and Philosophies for the Use of the Young.

*

It is pure unadulterated country life. They get up early because they have so much to do and go to bed early because they have so little to think about.
The Picture of Dorian Gray.

*

We are each our own devil, and we make this world our hell.
The Duchess of Padua.

*

Heaven is a despotism, I shall be at home there.
Vera, or The Nihilists.

*

Science can never grapple with the irrational. That is why it has no future before it, in this world. *An Ideal Husband.*

*

The world is a stage, but the play is badly cast.
Lord Arthur Savile's Crime.

I am always astonishing myself. It is the only thing that makes life worth living.   *A Woman of No Importance.*

*

The world is simply divided into two classes—those who believe the incredible, like the public—and those who do the improbable.   *A Woman of No Importance.*

*

The world has always laughed at its own tragedies, that being the only way in which it has been able to bear them.

A Woman of No Importance.

*

Memory is the diary that we all carry about with us.

The Importance of Being Earnest.

*

Discontent is the first step in the progress of a man or a nation.

A Woman of No Importance.

*

. . . anybody can be good in the country. There are no temptations there. That is the reason why people who live out of town are so absolutely uncivilized. Civilization is not by any means an easy thing to attain to. There are only two ways by which man can reach it. One is by being cultured, the other by being corrupt. Country people have no opportunity of being either, so they stagnate.   *The Picture of Dorian Gray.*

*

In Paris one can lose one's time most delightfully; but one can never lose one's way.   *In Conversation.*

*

Nowadays it is only the unreadable that occurs.

A Woman of No Importance.

*

On the Eiffel Tower:
Turn your back to that—you have all Paris before you. Look at it—Paris vanishes.   *In Conversation.*

One can survive everything nowadays, except death, and live down anything except a good reputation.

A Woman of No Importance.

*

Vulgarity and stupidity are two very vivid facts in modern life. One regrets them naturally. But there they are.

The Soul of Man Under Socialism.

*

Death and vulgarity are the only two facts in the nineteenth century that one cannot explain away.

The Picture of Dorian Gray.

*

Personally I cannot understand how anybody manages to exist in the country, if anybody who is anybody does. The country always bores me to death.

The Importance of Being Earnest.

*

But the past is of no importance. The present is of no importance. It is with the future that we have to deal. For the past is what man should not have been. The present is what man ought not to be. The future is what artists are.

The Soul of Man Under Socialism.

*

For he to whom the present is the only thing that is present, knows nothing of the age in which he lives.

In Conversation.

*

I wrote when I did not know life; now that I do know the meaning of life, I have no more to write. Life cannot be written; life can only be lived.　　　　*In Conversation.*

Why does not science, instead of troubling itself about sunspots, which nobody ever saw, or, if they did, ought not to speak about; why does not science busy itself with drainage and sanitary engineering. Why does it not clean the streets and free the rivers from pollutions?   *In Conversation. (America).*

*

Life is not complex. We are complex. Life is simple and the simple thing is the right thing.
                    Letter to Robert Ross from Reading Gaol.

*

...the world will not listen to me now. It is strange—I never thought it possible before—to regret that one has had too much leisure: leisure which I used so to lack, when I myself was a creator of beautiful things.   *In Conversation.*

*

... I wish to look at life, not to become a monument for tourists ... Privacy! ... I have had two years of it ... save for that other self the man I once was.   *Interview in Reading Gaol.*

*

Humanity takes itself too seriously. It is the world's original sin. If the cavemen had known how to laugh, History would have been different.   *In Conversation.*

*

In this world there are only two tragedies. One is not getting what one wants and the other is getting it.
                          Lady Windermere's Fan.

74

VI

LITERATURE

Oscar Wilde has justly earned for himself an undisputed place in English Literature, and with works completely dissimilar in character.

In his early days at Oxford he said, "I'll be a poet, a writer, a dramatist. Somehow or other I'll be famous, and if not famous I'll be notorious." His forecast was a true one in all respects.

Dr. Johnson's epitaph on Goldsmith, "He touched nothing he did not adorn," applies most aptly to the contributions of Oscar Wilde to Literature.

*

There is no such thing as a moral or an immoral book. Books are well written or badly written. That is all.

The Picture of Dorian Gray.

*

I never travel without my diary. One should always have something sensational to read in the train.

The Importance of Being Earnest.

*

The ancient historians gave us delightful fiction in the form of fact; the modern novelist presents us with dull facts under the guise of fiction. *The Decay of Lying.*

*

On Shakespeare:

In the spirit of the true artist, accepts the facts of the antiquarian and converts them into dramatic and picturesque effects.

The Truth of Masks.

*

M. Zola is determined to show that, if he has not got genius, he can at least be dull. *The Decay of Lying.*

Poor, silly, conceited Mr. Secretary Pepys has chattered his way into the circle of the Immortals.   *The Critic as Artist.*

*

M. GUY DE MAUPASSANT, with his keen mordant irony and his hard vivid style, strips life of the few poor rags that still cover her and shows us foul sore and festering wound. He writes lurid little tragedies in which everybody is ridiculous; bitter comedies at which one cannot laugh for very tears.

The Decay of Lying.

*

MR. RIDER HAGGARD, who really has, or had once, the makings of a perfectly magnificent liar, he is now so afraid of being suspected of genius that when he does tell anything marvellous, he feels bound to invent a personal reminiscence and to put it into a footnote as a kind of cowardly corroboration.

The Decay of Lying.

*

Only the great masters of style ever succeed in being obscure.
Phrases and Philosophies for the Use of the Young.

*

. . . in the works of our own Carlyle, whose *French Revolution* is one of the most fascinating historical novels ever written, facts are either kept in their subordinate position, or else entirely excluded on the general ground of dullness.

The Decay of Lying.

*

The cynic may mock at the subject of these verses, but we do not. Why not an ode on a knocker? Does not Victor Hugo's tragedy of Lucrece Borgia turn on the defacement of a door plate? Mr. Furlong must not be discouraged. Perhaps he will write poetry someday. If he does we would earnestly appeal to him to give up calling a cock "proud chanticleer."

Review in the Pall Mall Gazette.

Between them Hugo and Shakespeare have exhausted every subject. Originality is no longer possible—even in sin. So there are no real emotions left—only extraordinary adjectives.

In Conversation.

*

. . . it was to his blindness, as an occasion, if not as a cause, that England's great poet owed much of the majestic movement and sonorous splendour of his later verse. When Milton could no longer write he began to sing. *The Critic as Artist.*

*

WORDSWORTH went to the lakes, but he was never a lake poet. He found in stones the sermons he had already hidden there.

The Decay of Lying.

*

On Ruskin:
It was his prose I loved not his piety, his sympathy with the poor bored me. *In Conversation.*

*

On George Moore:
He leads his readers to the latrine and locks them in.

In Conversation.

*

MATTHEW ARNOLD, a fine but very mistaken poet, was always trying to do the most impossible thing of all—to know himself. And that is why sometimes, in the middle of his most beautiful poems, he left off being the poet and became the school inspector.

In Conversation.

*

MR. RUDYARD KIPLING—as one turns over the pages of his *Plain Tales from the Hills*, one feels as if one were seated under a palm-tree reading life by superb flashes of vulgarity. The bright colours of the bazaars dazzle one's eyes. The jaded, second-rate Anglo-Indians are in exquisite incongruity with their surroundings. The mere lack of style of the story-teller gives an old journalistic realism to what he tells us. From the point of view of life, he is a reporter who knows vulgarity better than any one has ever known it. Dickens knew its clothes and its comedy. Mr. Kipling knows its essence and its seriousness. He is our first authority on the second-rate and has seen marvellous things through keyholes, and his backgrounds are real works of art.

The Critic as Artist.

*

One incomparable novelist we have now in England, Mr. George Meredith. There are better artists in France, but France has no one whose view of life is so large, so varied, so imaginatively true. There are tellers of stories in Russia who have a more vivid sense of what pain in fiction may be. But to him belongs philosophy in fiction. His people not merely live, but they live in thought. One can see them from myriad points of view. They are suggestive. There is a soul in them and around them. They are interpretative and symbolic. And he who made them, those wonderful, quickly moving figures, made them for his own pleasure, and never asked the public what they wanted, has never cared to know what they wanted, has never allowed the public to dictate to him or influence him in any way, but has gone on intensifying his own personality, and producing his own individual work. At first none came to him. That did not matter. Then the few came to him. That did not change him. The many have come now. He is still the same. He is an incomparable novelist. *The Soul of Man Under Socialism.*

*

BALZAC—He was a most remarkable combination of the artistic temperament with the scientific spirit. A steady course of Balzac reduces our living friends to shadows, and our acquaintances to the shadow of the shades. *The Decay of Lying.*

*

MR. HALL CAINE, it is true, aims at the grandiose, but then he writes at the top of his voice. He is so loud that one cannot hear what he says. *The Decay of Lying.*

MR. ROBERT LOUIS STEVENSON, that delightful master of delicate and faithful prose. There is such a thing as robbing a story of its reality by trying to make it too true, and the *"Black Arrow"* is so inartistic as not to contain a single anachronism to boast of, while the transformation of Dr. Jekyll reads dangerously like an experiment out of *The Lancet*.   *The Decay of Lying.*

*

. . . poets . . . with the unfortunate exception of Mr. Wordsworth, have been really faithful to their high mission, and are universally recognized as being absolutely unreliable.

The Decay of Lying.

*

MR. HENRY JAMES, writes fiction as if it were a painful duty.

The Decay of Lying.

*

CHARLES READE, an artist, a scholar, a man with a true sense of beauty, raging and roaring over the abuses of contemporary life like a common pamphleteer or a sensational journalist, is really a sight for the angels to weep over.

The Decay of Lying.

*

GEORGE MEREDITH. His style is chaos illuminated by flashes of lightning. As a writer he has mastered everything except language : as a novelist he can do everything except tell a story : as an artist he is everything except articulate.

The Decay of Lying.

*

MR. JAMES PAYN is an adept in the art of concealing what is not worth finding.   *The Decay of Lying.*

*

ROBERT BROWNING : Yes, Browning was great. And as what will he be remembered? As a poet? Ah, not as a poet! He will be remembered as a writer of fiction, as the most supreme writer of fiction, it may be, that we have ever had. His sense of dramatic situation was unrivalled, and, if he could not answer his own problems, he could at least put problems forth, and what more should an artist do? Considered from the point of view of a creator of character he ranks next to him who made Hamlet. Had he been articulate, he might have sat beside him. The only man who can touch the hem of his garment is George Meredith. Meredith is a prose Browning, and so is Browning. He used poetry as a medium for writing in prose.   *The Critic as Artist.*

*

ROBERT BROWNING: He has been called a thinker, and was certainly a man who was always thinking, and always thinking aloud . . . So much, indeed did the subtle mechanism of mind fascinate him that he despised language, or looked upon it as an incomplete instrument of expression.   *The Critic as Artist.*

*

Shakespeare might have met Rozencratz and Guildenstern in the white streets of London, or seen the serving-men of rival houses bite their thumbs at each other in the open square; but Hamlet came out of his soul, and Romeo out of his passion.
                                              The Critic as Artist.

*

On being asked by a prison warder if Marie Corelli was a great writer:
Now don't think I've anything against her *moral* character, but from the way she writes she *ought to be in here.*
                                              In Conversation.

*

To call an artist morbid because he deals with morbidity as his subject-matter is as silly as if one called Shakespeare mad because he wrote *King Lear.*   *The Soul of Man Under Socialism.*

*

There are two ways of disliking poetry, one way is to dislike it, the other is to read Pope.   *In Conversation.*

A true artist takes no notice whatever of the public. The public to him are non-existent. He leaves that to the popular novelist.
The Soul of Man Under Socialism.

*

In literature mere egotism is delightful. It is what fascinates us in the letters of personalities so different as Cicero and Balzac, Flaubert and Berlioz, Byron and Madame de Sévigné. Whenever we came across it, and, strangely enough, it is rather rare, we cannot but welcome it.   *The Critic as Artist.*

*

They lead us through a barren desert of verbiage to a mirage that they call life . . . However, one should not be too severe on English novels; they are the only relaxation of the intellectually unemployed.   *Review in Pall Mall Gazette.*

*

For our own part . . . we cannot help expressing our regret that such a shallow and superficial biography as this should ever have been published. It is but a sorry task to rip the twisted ravel from the worn garment of life and to turn the grout into a drained cup.   *From " A Cheap Edition of a Great Man,"*
review in the Pall Mall Gazette.

*

Frank Harris tells that he was once asked to write a book of one hundred thousand words for some $5,000—in advance, by the American publishers *Harper's*. He wrote to them that as there were not one hundred thousand words in English he could not undertake the work.   *Reported by Frank Harris.*

*

The nineteenth century may be a prosaic age, but we fear that, if we are to judge by the general run of novels, it is not an age of prose.   *As a Reviewer.*

*

On Tree's Hamlet:
   . . . funny without being vulgar.   *In Conversation.*

The brilliant phrase like good wine, needs no bush. But just as the orator marks his good things by a dramatic pause, or by raising or lowering his voice, or by gesture, so the writer marks his epigrams with italics, setting the gems, as it were, like a jeweller —an excusable love of one's art, not all mere vanity, I like to think.   *In Conversation.*

                                        *

A great poet, a really great poet, is the most unpoetical of creatures. But inferior poets are absolutely fascinating. The worse their rhymes the more picturesque they look. The mere fact of having published a book of second-rate sonnets makes a man quite irresistible. He lives the poetry he cannot write. The others write the poetry that they dare not realize.
                                The Picture of Dorian Gray.

                                        *

I write because it gives me the greatest possible artistic pleasure to write. If my work pleases the few I am gratified. As for the mob, I have no desire to be a popular novelist. It is far too easy.   *Reply to a Critic.*

                                        *

All fine imaginative work is self-conscious and deliberate. No poet sings because he must sing. At least no great poet does. A great poet sings because he chooses to sing.
                                    The Critic as Artist.

                                        *

We fear that he will never produce any real good work till he has made up his mind whether destiny intends him for a poet or an advertising agent.   *As a Reviewer.*

                                        *

—can be read without any trouble and was probably written without any trouble also!   *As a Reviewer.*

                                        *

The author has written, as he says, "a tale without a murder," but having put a pistol-ball through his hero's chest and left him alive and hearty notwithstanding, he cannot be said to have produced a tale without a miracle.   *As a Reviewer.*

Medieval art is charming, but medieval emotions are out of date. One can use them in fiction, of course. But then the only things that one can use in fiction are the things that one has ceased to use in fact. *The Picture of Dorian Gray.*

*

. . . . a form of poetry which cannot possibly hurt anybody, even if translated into French.

Review in Pall Mall Gazette.

*

The nineteenth-century dislike of Realism is the rage of Caliban seeing his own face in a glass.

The nineteenth-century dislike of Romanticism is the rage of Caliban not seeing his own face in a glass.

The Picture of Dorian Gray.

*

"And now I must bid good-bye to your Excellent Aunt. I am due at the Athenaeum. It is the hour when we sleep there."

" All of you, Mr. Erskine? "

" Forty of us, in forty armchairs. We are practising for an English Academy of Letters." *The Picture of Dorian Gray.*

*

Literature always anticipates life. It does not copy it, but moulds it to its purpose. *The Decay of Lying.*

*

If one cannot enjoy reading a book over and over again, there is no use in reading it at all. *The Decay of Lying.*

*

I quite admit that modern novels have many good points. All I insist on is that, as a class, they are quite unreadable.

The Decay of Lying.

*

Romantic surroundings are the worst surroundings possible for a romantic writer.

Letter to Robert Ross written from Reading Gaol.

We have been able to have fine poetry in England because the
public do not read it, and consequently do not influence it.
The Soul of Man Under Socialism.

*

The books that the world calls immoral books are books that
show the world its own shame.   *The Picture of Dorian Gray.*

*

On Charles Dickens:
One must have a heart of stone to read the death of Little Nell
without laughing.   *In Conversation.*

*

I dislike modern memoirs. They are generally written by
people who have entirely lost their memories, or have never done
anything worth remembering; which, however, is, no doubt,
the true explanation of their popularity, as the English public
always feels perfectly at its ease when a mediocrity is talking to it.
The Critic as Artist.

*

Anybody can write a three-volumed novel.   It merely requires
a complete ignorance of both life and literature.
The Critic as Artist.

*

To know the vintage and quality of a wine one need not drink
the whole cask.   It must be perfectly easy in half an hour to say
whether a book is worth anything or worth nothing.   Ten
minutes are really sufficient, if one has the instinct for form.
Who wants to wade through a dull volume?   One tastes it, and
that is quite enough.   *The Critic as Artist.*

*

In point of fact, there is no such thing as Shakespeare's Hamlet.
If Hamlet has something of the definiteness of a work of art, he
has also all the obscurity that belongs to life.   There are as many
Hamlets as there are melancholies.   *The Critic as Artist.*

But there is no literary public in England for anything except newspapers, primers and encyclopædias. Of all the people in the world the English have the least sense of the beauty of literature. *The Picture of Dorian Gray.*

*

The popular novel that the public call healthy is always a thoroughly unhealthy production; and what the public call an unhealthy novel is always a beautiful and healthy work of art. *The Soul of Man Under Socialism.*

*

I hate vulgar realism in literature. The man who could call a spade a spade should be compelled to use one. It is the only thing he is fit for. *The Picture of Dorian Gray.*

*

There is not a single real poet or prose writer of this century, on whom the British public have not solemnly conferred diplomas of immorality, and these diplomas practically take the place, with us, of what in France is the formal recognition of an Academy of Letters, and fortunately make the establishment of such an institution quite unnecessary in England. *The Soul of Man Under Socialism.*

*

On a book by four authors:
It has taken four people to write it and even to read it requires assistance. It is a book that one can with perfect safety recommend to other people. *As a Reviewer.*

*

The aim of most of our modern novelists seems to be, not to write good novels, but to write novels that will do good. *As a Reviewer.*

*

When the public say a work is grossly unintelligible, they mean that the artist has said or made a beautiful thing that is new; when they describe a work as grossly immoral, they mean that the artist has said or made a beautiful thing that is true. *The Soul of Man Under Socialism.*

85

It is a curious fact that the worst work is always done with the best intentions, and that people are never so trivial as when they take themselves very seriously. *As a Reviewer.*

*

We sincerely hope that a few more novels like these will be published, as the public will then find out that a bad book is very dear at a shilling. *As a Reviewer.*

*

Russian writers are extraordinary. What makes their books so great is the pity they put into them. *In Conversation.*

*

I appropriate what is already mine, for once a thing is published it becomes public property. *In Conversation.*

*

There are two ways of disliking my plays, one way is to dislike them, the other is to prefer *Earnest.* *In Conversation.*

*

"Dry-goods! What are American dry-goods?" asked the Duchess, raising her large hands in wonder, and accentuating the verb.

"American novels," answered Lord Henry, helping himself to some quail. *The Picture of Dorian Gray.*

*

Poets know how useful passion is for publication. Nowadays a broken heart will run to many editions.

The Picture of Dorian Gray.

*

A poet can survive anything but a misprint.

In Conversation.

*

Literature always anticipates life. It does not copy it, but moulds it to its purpose. The nineteenth century, as we know it, is largely an invention of Balzac. *The Decay of Lying.*

86

The Importance of Being Earnest:
The first act is ingenious, the second beautiful, the third abominably clever. *In Conversation.*

*

I am sure you must have a great future in literature before you . . . because you seem to be such a very bad interviewer. I feel sure that you must write poetry. I certainly like the colour of your necktie very much. Goodbye. *In an Interview.*

*

No modern literary work of any worth has been produced in the English language by an English writer—except of course Bradshaw. *In Conversation.*

*

The basis of literary friendship is mixing the poisoned bowl. *In Conversation.*

*

—there is a great deal to be said in favour of reading a novel backwards. The last page is, as a rule, the most interesting and when one begins with the catastrophe or the *dénouement* one feels on pleasant terms of equality with the author. It is like going behind the scenes of a theatre. One is no longer taken in, and the hairbreadth escapes of the hero and the wild agonies of the heroine leave one absolutely unmoved. *In Conversation.*

*

K. E. V.'s little volume is a series of poems on the Saints. Each poem is preceded by a brief biography of the Saint it celebrates—which is a very necessary precaution, as few of them ever existed. It does not display much poetic power and such lines as these on St. Stephen . . . may be said to add another horror to martyrdom. Still it is a thoroughly well-intentioned book and eminently suitable for invalids. *As a Reviewer.*

VII

MUSIC

Oscar Wilde's knowledge and appreciation of music was very limited, and when he occasionally introduced his theories into his conversation it was merely to add to the picture of himself as the complete artist.

He was once asked by a fond mother, whose daughter was playing the piano, whether he liked music.

Oscar said: " No, but I like that! "

*

. . . if one plays good music people don't listen, and if one plays bad music people don't talk.

The Importance of Being Earnest.

*

The typewriting machine, when played with expression, is not more annoying than the piano when played by a sister or near relation. Indeed, many among those most devoted to domesticity prefer it.

Letter to Robert Ross written from Reading Prison.

*

LORD HENRY: You must play Chopin to me. The man with whom my wife ran away played Chopin exquisitely.

The Picture of Dorian Gray.

*

After playing Chopin, I feel as if I had been weeping over sins that I had never committed, and mourning over tragedies that were not my own. Music always seems to me to produce that effect. It creates for one a past of which one has been ignorant and fills one with a sense of sorrows that have been hidden from one's tears. *The Critic as Artist.*

Music makes one feel so romantic—at least it always got on one's nerves—which is the same thing nowadays.

A Woman of No Importance.

*

Musical people are so absurdly unreasonable. They always want one to be perfectly dumb at the very moment when one is longing to be absolutely deaf.   *An Ideal Husband.*

*

I don't play accurately—anyone can play accurately—but I play with wonderful expression. As far as the piano is concerned, sentiment is my *forte*. I keep science for life.

The Importance of Being Earnest.

*

I like Wagner's music better than anybody's. It is so loud that one can talk the whole time without people hearing what one says.

The Picture of Dorian Gray.

VIII

PARENTS

Wilde's parents were people of considerable importance in Dublin. His father, William Wilde, knighted in 1864, was a great and internationally famous oculist and surgeon. He was a small, vigorous man, addicted to hard drinking and was excessively interested in sexual exploits with young women. Owing to his lusty, uninhibited way of life he was constantly in trouble with girls and his activities resulted in many unwanted offspring. Despite the many scandals in which he became involved Sir William retained his reputation as a man of intellectual distinction and a brilliant surgeon, until his death in 1887.

Oscar Wilde's mother, whose maiden name was Jane Elgee, was twenty-eight and her husband thirty-nine when Oscar was born. Lady Wilde was a tall, stately, imposing woman, talented and eccentric. As a young woman she wrote for a revolutionary newspaper under the nom de plume of " Speranza."

She was a clever talker with a rich, eloquent voice, and her " At Homes " were occasions of importance in Dublin society.

Oscar had little in common with his father and a great deal in common with his mother, whom he resembled in looks, voice, and eccentricities.

*

Few parents nowadays pay any regard to what their children say to them. The old-fashioned respect for the young is fast dying. *The Importance of Being Earnest.*

*

Children begin by loving their parents. After a time they judge them. Rarely, if ever do they forgive them.
A Woman of No Importance.

All women become like their mothers. That is their tragedy. No man does. That's his.

The Importance of Being Earnest.

＊

To lose one parent . . . may be regarded as a misfortune; to lose both looks like carelessness.

The Importance of Being Earnest.

＊

To a fellow undergraduate at Trinity College:
Come home with me, I want to introduce you to my mother. We have founded a society for the suppression of Virtue.

In Conversation.

＊

Fathers should neither be seen nor heard. That is the only proper basis for family life.   *An Ideal Husband.*

＊

The longer I live the more keenly I feel that whatever was good enough for our fathers is not good enough for us.

The Picture of Dorian Gray.

＊

A mother's love is very touching, of course, but it is often curiously selfish. I mean, there is a good deal of selfishness in it.

A Woman of No Importance.

＊

Why will parents always appear at the wrong time? Some extraordinary mistake in nature, I suppose.

An Ideal Husband.

＊

I should imagine that most mothers don't quite understand their sons.   *A Woman of No Importance.*

＊

I was influenced by my mother. Every man is when he is young.   *A Woman of No Importance.*

She was a wonderful woman, and such a feeling as vulgar jealousy could take no hold on her. She was well aware of my father's constant infidelities, but simply ignored them. Before my father died, in 1876, he lay ill in bed for many days. And every morning a woman dressed in black and closely veiled used to come to our house in Merrion Square, and unhindered either by my mother or anyone else used to walk straight upstairs to Sir William's bedroom and sit down at the head of his bed, and so sit there all day, without ever speaking a word or once raising her veil.

She took no notice of anybody in the room, and nobody paid any attention to her. Not one woman in a thousand would have tolerated her presence, but my mother allowed it, because she knew that my father loved this woman and felt that it must be a joy and a comfort to have her there by his dying bed. And I am sure that she did right not to judge that last happiness of a man who was about to die, and I am sure that my father understood her apparent indifference, understood that it was not because she did not love him that she permitted her rival's presence, but because she loved him very much, and died with his heart full of gratitude and affection for her.

Oscar Wilde's tribute to his mother.

IX

MARRIAGE

Oscar Wilde was married to Constance Mary Lloyd, the only child of an eminent and wealthy barrister, on May 29th 1884. They had two sons, Cyril and Vyvyan born in 1885 and 1886 respectively.

At first they were passionately in love and indeed Constance maintained her affections until the end. It was an attraction of opposites and Wilde was once asked how he came to fall in love with his wife. He replied: " She never speaks and I am always wondering what her thoughts are like."

Wilde was ill-suited for the role of domesticity and for a time it was rumoured that he was in love with an actress. Once when the actress was on tour he spent a week away from home. On his return he was describing, with poetic eloquence, the mansion he had visited to a group of enchanted listeners, when Constance asked quietly, "Did she act well, Oscar?"

*

Men marry because they are tired; women because they are curious; both are disappointed.   *The Picture of Dorian Gray.*

*

The one charm of marriage is that it makes a life of deception absolutely necessary for both parties.

The Picture of Dorian Gray.

*

The real drawback to marriage is that it makes one unselfish. And unselfish people are colourless.

The Picture of Dorian Gray.

93

Of course married life is merely a habit, a bad habit. But then one regrets the loss of even one's worst habits. Perhaps one regrets them the most. They are such an essential part of one's personality. *The Picture of Dorian Gray.*

*

I have often observed that in married households the champagne is rarely of a first-rate brand.
The Importance of Being Earnest.

*

There is one thing worse than an absolutely loveless marriage. A marriage in which there is love, but on one side only.
An Ideal Husband.

*

I am not in favour of long engagements. They give people the opportunity of finding out each other's character before marriage, which I think is never advisable.
The Importance of Being Earnest.

*

The amount of women in London who flirt with their own husbands is perfectly scandalous. It looks so bad. It is simply washing one's clean linen in public.
The Importance of Being Earnest.

*

The happiness of a married man depends on the people he has not married. *A Woman of No Importance.*

*

If we men married the women we deserve we should have a very bad time of it. *An Ideal Husband.*

*

How can a woman be expected to be happy with a man who insists on treating her as if she were a perfectly natural being.
A Woman of No Importance.

It's most dangerous nowadays for a husband to pay any attention to his wife in public. It always makes people think that he beats her when they're alone.

Lady Windermere's Fan.

*

MRS. ALLONBY : My husband is a sort of promissory note; I'm tired of meeting him. *A Woman of No Importance.*

*

Marriage is hardly a thing that one can do now and then— except in America. *The Picture of Dorian Gray.*

*

For an artist to marry his model is as fatal as for a *gourmet* to marry his cook : the one gets no sittings, and the other no dinner.

In Conversation.

*

Polygamy—how much more poetic it is to marry one and love many. *In Conversation.*

*

No man should have a secret from his wife—she invariably finds it out. *In Conversation.*

*

A family is a terrible encumbrance, especially when one is not married. *Vera, or The Nihilists.*

*

Twenty years of romance make a woman look like a ruin; but twenty years of marriage make her look like a public building.

A Woman of No Importance.

*

In married life affection comes when people thoroughly dis- like each other. *An Ideal Husband.*

*

It is the growth of the moral sense in women that makes marriage such a hopeless one-sided institution.

An Ideal Husband.

LADY MARKBY : We might drive in the Park at five. Everything looks so fresh in the Park now!

MRS. CHEVELEY : Except the people!

LADY MARKBY : Perhaps the people are a little jaded. I have often observed that the Season as it goes on produces a kind of softening of the brain. However, I think anything is better than high intellectual pressure. That is the most unbecoming thing there is. It makes the noses of the young girls so particularly large. And there is nothing so difficult to marry as a large nose.

An Ideal Husband.

*

LORD AUGUSTUS : . . . It is a great thing to come across a woman who thoroughly understands one.

DUMBY : It is an awfully dangerous thing. They always end by marrying one.　　　　　　　　　　　　*Lady Windermere's Fan.*

*

LADY CAROLINE : . . . women have become so highly educated . . . that nothing should surprise us nowadays, except happy marriages. They apparently are getting very rare.

MRS. ALLONBY : Oh, they're quite out of date.

LADY STUTFIELD : Except amongst the middle classes, I have been told.

MRS. ALLONBY : How like the middle classes!

A Woman of No Importance.

*

How marriage ruins a man! It's as demoralizing as cigarettes, and far more expensive.　　　　　　　　　*Lady Windermere's Fan.*

*

Englishwomen conceal their feelings till after they are married. They show them then.　　　　　　　　*A Woman of No Importance.*

*

DUKE : . . . I have noted
How merry is that husband by whose hearth
Sits an uncomely wife.　　　　　　　　　*The Duchess of Padua.*

. . . in married life three is company and two is none.
The Importance of Being Earnest.

*

I have always been of the opinion that a man who desires to get married should know either everything or nothing.
The Importance of Being Earnest.

*

The proper basis for marriage is mutual misunderstanding.
Lord Arthur Savile's Crime.

*

LADY MARKBY : . . . In my time . . . we were taught not to understand anything. That was the old system, and wonderfully interesting it was. I assure you that the amount of things I and my poor sister were taught not to understand was quite extraordinary. But modern women understand everything, I am told.
MRS. CHEVELEY : Except their husbands. That is the one thing the modern woman never understands.
LADY MARKBY : And a very good thing too, dear, I dare say. It might break up many a happy home if they did.
An Ideal Husband.

*

. . . to elope is cowardly. It's running away from danger. And danger has become so rare in modern life.
A Woman of No Importance.

*

As for domesticity, it ages one rapidly, and distracts one's mind from higher things. *The Remarkable Rocket.*

*

Nowadays all the married men are like bachelors, and all the bachelors like married men. *The Picture of Dorian Gray.*

*

When a woman finds out about her husband she either becomes dreadfully dowdy, or wears very smart bonnets that some other woman's husband has to pay for.
The Picture of Dorian Gray.

97

All men are married women's property. That is the only true definition of what married women's property really is.

A Woman of No Importance.

*

Her capacity for family affection is extraordinary. When her third husband died, her hair turned quite gold from grief.

The Picture of Dorian Gray.

*

On seeing Tree in a play (" Once Upon a Time ")

Since the appearance of Tree in pyjamas—there has been the greatest sympathy for Mrs. Tree. It throws a lurid light on the difficulties of their married life.   *In Correspondence.*

*

There is no pleasure in taking in a husband who never sees anything.   *The Picture of Dorian Gray.*

*

When a woman marries again, it is because she detested her first husband. When a man marries again, it is because he adored his first wife. Women try their luck; men risk theirs.

The Picture of Dorian Gray.

*

MRS. ALLONBY : The Ideal Husband? There couldn't be such a thing. The institution is wrong.

A Woman of No Importance.

*

DUCHESS OF BERWICK : Our husbands would really forget our existence if we didn't nag at them from time to time, just to remind them that we have a perfect legal right to do so.

Lady Windermere's Fan.

*

It is a curious thing about the game of marriage—the wives hold all the honours, and invariably lose the odd trick.

Lady Windermere's Fan.

Secrets from other people's wives are a necessary luxury in modern life. So, at least, I am always told at the club by people who are old enough to know better. *An Ideal Husband.*

*

There's nothing in the world like the devotion of a married woman. It's a thing no married man knows anything about.
Lady Windermere's Fan.

*

MRS. ALLONBY : When Ernest and I were engaged, he swore to me positively on his knees that he never loved anyone before in the whole course of his life. I was very young at the time, so I didn't believe him, I needn't tell you. Unfortunately, however, I made no enquiries of any kind till after I had been actually married four or five months. I found out then that what he had told me was perfectly true. And that sort of thing makes a man so uninteresting. *A Woman of No Importance.*

X

LOVE

In his youth he had a young man's normal interest in girls. When he married he was passionately in love with his wife, and once caused acute embarrassment to a friend by describing in unnecessary detail the physical pleasures of his marriage.

Later women ceased to attract him, and in 1889, he commenced the course of conduct that led to his downfall.

*

It is difficult not to be unjust to what one loves.
The Critic as Artist.

*

Love is an illusion.   *The Picture of Dorian Gray.*

*

Nothing spoils a romance so much as a sense of humour in the woman—or the want of it in the man.
A Woman of No Importance.

*

The worst of having a romance of any kind is that it leaves one so unromantic.   *The Picture of Dorian Gray.*

*

PRINCE PAUL: . . . You want a new excitement, Prince. Let me see—you have been married twice already suppose you try— falling in love for once.   *Vera, or The Nihilists.*

*

They do not sin at all
Who sin for love.
The Duchess of Padua.

I might mimic a passion that I do not feel, but I cannot mimic one that burns one like fire.

The Picture of Dorian Gray.

*

. . . not love at first sight, but love at the end of the season, which is so much more satisfactory.   *Lady Windermere's Fan.*

*

. . . life cannot be understood without much charity, cannot be lived without much charity. It is love, and not German philosophy, that is the true explanation of this world, whatever may be the explanation of the next.   *An Ideal Husband.*

*

Oxford is the capital of Romance . . . in its own way as memorable as Athens and to me it was even more entrancing.

In Conversation.

*

Love can canonize people. The saints are those who have been most loved.   *Letter to Robert Ross, May 28th 1897.*

*

There is always something ridiculous about the emotions of people whom one has ceased to love.

The Picture of Dorian Gray.

*

There are romantic memories, and there is the desire for romance—that is all. Our most fiery moments of ecstasy are merely shadows of what somewhere else we have felt, or of what we long some day to feel.   *In Conversation.*

*

MRS. ALLONBY : There is a beautiful moon tonight.
LORD ILLINGWORTH : Let us go and look at it. To look at anything that is inconstant is charming nowadays.

A Woman of No Importance.

Keep love in your heart. A life without it is like a sunless garden when the flowers are dead. The consciousness of loving and being loved brings a warmth and richness to life that nothing else can bring.   *In Conversation.*

*

One should always be in love. That is the reason one should never marry.   *In Conversation.*

*

. . . a really *grande passion* is comparatively rare nowadays. It is the privilege of people who have nothing to do. That is the one use of the idle classes in a country.
                                                A Woman of No Importance.

*

The real Don Juan is not the vulgar person who goes about making love to all the women he meets, and what the novelists call "seducing" them. The real Don Juan is the man who says to women "Go away! I don't want you. You interfere with my life. I can do without you." Swift was the real Don Juan. Two women died for him!   *In Conversation.*

*

Any place you love is the world to you . . . but love is not fashionable any more, the poets have killed it. They wrote so much about it that nobody believed them, and I am not surprised. True love suffers, and is silent.   *The Remarkable Rocket.*

*

. . . love and gluttony justify everything.   *In Conversation.*

*

To love oneself is the beginning of a life-long romance.
                Phrases and Philosophies for the Use of the Young.

*

Faithfulness is to the emotional life what consistency is to the life of the intellect—simply a confession of failure.
                                                In Conversation.

There is so much else to do in the world but love.
Vera, or The Nihilists.

*

Men always want to be a woman's first love. That is their clumsy vanity. Women have a more subtle instinct about things : What they like is to be a man's last romance.
A Woman of No Importance.

*

What a silly thing love is ! It is not half as useful as logic, for it does not prove anything and it is always telling one things that are not going to happen, and making one believe things that are not true. *The Nightingale and the Rose.*

*

Ouida loved Lord Lytton with a love that made his life a burden. *In Conversation.*

*

Romance is the privilege of the rich, not the profession of the poor. *The Model Millionaire.*

*

Nothing is serious except passion. The intellect is not a serious thing, and never has been. It is an instrument on which one plays, that is all. *A Woman of No Importance.*

*

It is said that passion makes one think in a circle.
The Picture of Dorian Gray.

*

Chiromancy is a most dangerous science, and one that ought not to be encouraged, except in a *tête-à-tête*.
Lord Arthur Savile's Crime.

*

Romance should never begin with sentiment. It should begin with science and end with a settlement. *An Ideal Husband.*

The very essence of romance is uncertainty. If ever I get married, I'll certainly try to forget the fact.
The Importance of Being Earnest.

*

Once a week is quite enough to propose to anyone, and it should always be done in a manner that attracts some attention.
An Ideal Husband.

*

It is not the perfect but the imperfect who have need of love.
An Ideal Husband.

*

I am not at all romantic. I am not old enough. I leave romance to my seniors.
An Ideal Husband.

*

A kiss may ruin a human life.   *A Woman of No Importance.*

*

If one really loves a woman, all other women in the world become absolutely meaningless to one.
Lady Windermere's Fan.

*

Who, being loved, is poor?   *A Woman of No Importance.*

*

Romance lives by repetition, and repetition converts an appetite into an art. Besides each tune one loves is the only tune one has loved. Difference of object does not alter singleness of passion.   *The Picture of Dorian Gray.*

*

DUCHESS OF MONMOUTH: . . . We women, as someone says, love with our ears, just as you men love with your eyes, if you ever love at all.   *The Picture of Dorian Gray.*

*

A man can be happy with any woman as long as he does not love her.   *The Picture of Dorian Gray.*

When one is in love one begins by deceiving oneself. And ends by deceiving others. That is what the world calls a romance.   *A Woman of No Importance.*

*

Those who are faithful know only the trivial side of love : it is the faithless who know love's tragedies.
                    The Picture of Dorian Gray.

*

Faithfulness is to the emotional life what consistency is to the life of the intellect—simply a confession of failures.
                    The Picture of Dorian Gray.

*

Young men want to be faithful and are not; old men want to be faithless and cannot.   *The Picture of Dorian Gray.*

*

Always! That is a dreadful word. It makes me shudder when I hear it. Women are so fond of using it. They spoil every romance by trying to make it last for ever. It is a meaning-less word too. The only difference between a caprice and a life-long passion is that the caprice lasts a little longer.
                    The Picture of Dorian Gray.

*

The people who have adored me—there have not been very many, but there have been some—have always insisted on living on, long after I have ceased to care for them, or they to care for me.   *The Picture of Dorian Gray.*

XI

RELIGION

During his early travels in Italy, he was impressed by the ceremony and pageantry of the Catholic Church, and expressed his admiration of the Catholic faith. Paradoxically, later he became a Freemason.

In 1900, when in Rome, he was blessed by the Pope, not once, but seven times, although it was not until he lay dying that he was converted, but he died as he lived, a pagan.

*

It is the confession, not the priest that gives us absolution.
The Picture of Dorian Gray.

*

Religion is the fashionable substitute for Belief.
The Picture of Dorian Gray.

*

There is no thing more precious than a human soul, nor any earthly thing that can be weighed with it.
The Model Millionaire.

*

Prayer must never be answered : if it is, it ceases to be prayer and becomes correspondence.   *In Conversation.*

*

Most religious teachers spend their time trying to prove the unproven by the unprovable.   *In Conversation.*
*

Religions . . . may be absorbed, but they are never disproved.
The Rise of Historical Criticism.

To die for one's theological beliefs is the worst use a man can make of his life.   *The Portrait of Mr. W. H.*

*

Through the streets of Jerusalem at the present day crawls one who is mad and carries a wooden cross on his shoulders. He is a symbol of the lives that are marred by imitation.
The Soul of Man Under Socialism.

*

A sermon is a sorry sauce when you have nothing to eat it with.
The Duchess of Padua.

*

LADY HUNSTANTON : . . . there was . . . I remember, a clergyman who wanted to be a lunatic, or a lunatic who wanted to be a clergyman, I forget which, but I know the Court of Chancery investigated the matter, and decided he was quite sane. And I saw him afterwards at poor Lord Plumstead's with straws in his hair, or something very odd about him.
A Woman of No Importance.

*

I hope to be in Rome in about 10 days—and this time I really must become a Catholic—though I fear that if I went before the Holy Father with a blossoming rod it would turn at once into an umbrella or something dreadful of that kind. It is absurd to say that the age of miracles is past. It has not yet begun.
Letter from Paris, 1900.

*

. . . it is rarely in the world's history that its ideal has been one of joy and beauty. The worship of pain has far more often dominated the world. Medievalism, with its saints and martyrs, its love of self-torture, its wild passion for wounding itself, its gashing with knives, and its whipping with rods— Medievalism is real Christianity and the medieval Christ is the real Christ.   *The Soul of Man Under Socialism.*

People fashion their God after their own understanding. They make their God first and worship him afterwards. I should advise you however to postpone coming to any conclusion at present; and if you should happen to die in the meantime, you will stand a much better chance, should a future exist, than some of these braying parsons.

*To a Convict who confessed to the
uncertainty of his religious belief.*

*

"Nay but God careth for the sparrows even, and feedeth them," he answered.

"Do not the sparrows die of hunger in the winter?" she asked. "And is it not winter now?" And the man answered nothing, but stirred not from the threshold.   *The Star Child.*

*

Scepticism is the beginning of Faith.

The Picture of Dorian Gray.

*

In a Temple everyone should be serious, except the thing that is worshipped.   *A Woman of No Importance.*

*

Religions die when they are proved to be true.   Science is the record of dead religions.

Phrases and Philosophies for the Use of the Young.

*

Missionaries, my dear! Don't you realize that missionaries are the divinely provided food for destitute and underfed cannibals? Whenever they are on the brink of starvation, Heaven in its infinite mercy sends them a nice plump missionary.

In Conversation.

*

To the wickedness of the Papacy humanity owes much. The goodness of the Papacy owes a terrible debt to humanity.

The Soul of Man Under Socialism.

We came to Rome on Holy Thursday—I appeared in the front rank of the Pilgrims in the Vatican, and got the blessing of the Holy Father—a blessing they would have denied me.

He was wonderful as he was carried past me on his throne—not of flesh and blood—but a white soul robed in white—and an artist as well as a saint—the only instance in History, if the newspapers are to be believed.

I have seen nothing like the extraordinary grace of his gesture, as he rose from moment to moment, to bless—possibly the pilgrims but certainly me. Tree should see him. It is his only chance.

I was deeply impressed, and my walking-stick showed signs of budding; would have budded indeed, only at the door of the Chapel it was taken from me by the Knave of Spades. This strange prohibition is, of course, in honour of Tannhaüser.

How did I get a ticket? By a miracle, of course. I thought it was hopeless and made no effort of any kind. On Saturday afternoon at 5 o'clock Harold and I went to have tea at the Hôtel de l'Europe. Suddenly, as I was eating buttered toast, a man, or what seemed to be one, dressed like a Hotel Porter entered and asked me would I like to see the Pope on Easter Day. I bowed my head humbly and said " Non sum dignus ", or words to that effect. He at once produced a ticket!

When I tell you that his countenance was of supernatural ugliness, and that the price of the ticket was thirty pieces of silver, I need say no more.

An equally curious thing is that whenever I pass the Hotel, which I do constantly I see the same man. Scientists call that phenomenon an obsession of the visual nerve. You and I know better.   *Letter to Robert Ross from Rome, April 16, 1900.*

XII

CONDUCT

To Wilde manners were more important than morals. On the few occasions when he spoke unkindly it was usually to correct bad manners in others. On one occasion an exuberant nobleman clapped Wilde on the back whilst he was speaking, and said, " Why, Oscar, you are getting fatter and fatter! " Wilde replied, without looking round, " And you are getting ruder and ruder."

*

Any preoccupation with ideas of what is right or wrong in conduct shows an arrested intellectual development.
Phrases and Philosophies for the use of the Young.

*

To be natural is such a very difficult pose to keep up.
An Ideal Husband.

*

Let me say to you now that to do nothing at all is the most difficult thing in the world, the most difficult, and the most intellectual. *The Critic as Artist.*

*

A sensitive person is one who, because he has corns himself, always treads on other people's toes.
The Remarkable Rocket.

*

What people call insincerity is simply a method by which we can multiply our personalities. *The Critic as Artist.*

*

. . . my duty is a thing I never do, on principle.
An Ideal Husband.

The only thing that ever consoles man for the stupid things he does is the praise he always gives himself for doing them.

In Conversation.

*

If we lived long enough to see the results of our actions it may be that those who call themselves good would be sickened with a dull remorse, and those whom the world calls evil stirred by a noble joy. *The Critic as Artist.*

*

Conscience and cowardice are really the same things. Conscience is the trade-name of the firm.

The Picture of Dorian Gray.

*

A cynic is a man who knows the price of everything and the value of nothing. *Lady Windermere's Fan.*

*

To be either a Puritan, a prig or a preacher is a bad thing. To be all three at once reminds me of the worst excesses of the French Revolution. *Letter from Paris, June 1898.*

*

. . . duty is what one expects from others, it is not what one does oneself. *A Woman of No Importance.*

*

Nothing looks so like innocence as an indiscretion.

Lord Arthur Savile's Crime.

*

All bad poetry springs from genuine feeling. To be natural is to be obvious, and to be obvious is to be inartistic.

The Critic as Artist.

*

Moderation is a fatal thing. Nothing succeeds like excess.

A Woman of No Importance.

Nothing is so dangerous as being too modern. One is apt to grow old-fashioned quite suddenly.   *An Ideal Husband.*

*

It is often said that force is no argument. That, however, entirely depends on what one wants to prove.
                    The Soul of Man under Socialism.

*

Actions are the first tragedy in life, words are the second. Words are perhaps the worst. Words are merciless.
                    Lady Windermere's Fan.

*

Philanthropy seems to me to have become simply the refuge of people who wish to annoy their fellow creatures.
                    An Ideal Husband.

*

The basis of every scandal is an immoral certainty.
                    The Picture of Dorian Gray.

*

The one advantage of playing with fire is that one never gets even singed. It is the people who don't know how to play with it who get burned up.   *A Woman of No Importance.*

*

When we are happy we are always good but when we are good we are not always happy.   *In Conversation.*

*

There is no such thing as a good influence. All influence is immoral—immoral from the scientific point of view.
                    The Picture of Dorian Gray.

*

To be good is to be in harmony with oneself. Discord is to be forced to be in harmony with others.   *In Conversation.*

Everyone should keep someone else's diary.
In Conversation.

*

Whenever a man does a thoroughly stupid thing, it is always from the noblest of motives.　*The Picture of Dorian Gray.*

*

A little sincerity is a dangerous thing, and a great deal of it is absolutely fatal.　*The Critic as Artist.*

*

There is a fatality about good resolutions—they are always made too late.　*The Picture of Dorian Gray.*

*

One should always play fairly—when one has the winning cards.　*An Ideal Husband.*

*

Being natural is simply a pose, and the most irritating pose I know.　*The Picture of Dorian Gray.*

*

Your handwriting in your last was so dreadful that it looked as if you were writing a three volume novel on the terrible spread of communistic ideas among the rich, or in some other way wasting a youth that has always been, and always will remain, quite full of promise.
*Reply to a letter from Robert Ross,
written from Reading Prison.*

*

A good reputation is one of the many annoyances to which I have never been subjected.　*A Woman of No Importance.*

*

I don't like principles . . . I prefer prejudices.
An Ideal Husband.

113

No crime is vulgar, but all vulgarity is crime.   Vulgarity is
the conduct of others.
                    Phrases and Philosophies for the Use of the Young.

*

You never say a moral thing, and you never do a wrong thing.
Your cynicism is simply a pose.   *The Picture of Dorian Gray.*

*

. . . it is so easy to convert others.   It is so difficult to convert
oneself.   *The Critic as Artist.*

*

It is only the superficial qualities that last.   Man's deeper
nature is soon found out.
                    Phrases and Philosophies for the Use of the Young.

*

. . . all influence is bad, but a good influence is the worst in the
world.   *A Woman of No Importance.*

*

Optimism begins in a broad grin, and Pessimism ends with
blue spectacles.   *An Ideal Husband.*

*

I rely on you to misrepresent me.   *In Conversation.*

*

I am but too conscious of the fact that we are born in an age
when only the dull are treated seriously, and I live in terror of
not being misunderstood.   *The Critic as Artist.*

*

A temperament capable of receiving, through an imaginative
medium, and under imaginative conditions, new and beautiful
impressions, is the only temperament that can be a work of art.
                    The Soul of Man Under Socialism.

114

What are the unreal things, but the passions that once burned like fire? What are the incredible things, but the things that one has faithfully believed? What are the improbable things? The things that one has done oneself.   *The Critic as Artist.*

*

Moderation is a fatal thing. Enough is as bad as a meal. More than enough is as good as a feast.
                                        The Picture of Dorian Gray.

*

The prig is a very interesting psychological study, and though of all poses a moral pose is the most offensive, still to have a pose at all is something.   *The Critic as Artist.*

I never put off till tomorrow what I can possibly do—the day after.   *In Conversation.*

*

They say a good lawyer can break the law as often as he likes, and no one can say him nay. If a man knows the law he knows his duty.   *Vera, or The Nihilists.*

*

To be premature is to be perfect.
                        Phrases and Philosophies for the Use of the Young.

*

I think everyone should have their hands told once a month so as to know what not to do.   *Lord Arthur Savile's Crime.*

*

It is always more difficult to destroy than to create, and when what one has to destroy is vulgarity and stupidity, the task of destruction needs not merely courage but also contempt.
                                        The Critic as Artist.

*

It is quite remarkable how one good action always breeds another.   *The Devoted Friend.*

He would stab his best friend for the sake of writing an epigram on his tombstone.   *Vera, or The Nihilists.*

*

For a house lacking a host is but an empty thing and void of honour.   *A Florentine Tragedy.*

*

The first duty in life is to be as artificial as possible. What the second duty is no one has yet discovered.
Phrases and Philosophies for the Use of the Young.

*

Dullness is the coming-of-age of seriousness.
Phrases and Philosophies for the Use of the Young.

*

A publicist, nowadays, is a man who bores the community with the details of the illegalities of his private life.
Pen, Pencil and Poison.

*

Every effect that one produces gives one an enemy. To be popular one must be a mediocrity.
The Picture of Dorian Gray.

*

It is always nice to be expected and not to arrive.
An Ideal Husband.

*

One should always be a little improbable.
Phrases and Philosophies for the Use of the Young.

*

There *is* a good deal to be said for blushing, if one can do it at the proper moment.   *A Woman of No Importance.*

*

Perhaps one never seems so much at one's ease as when one has to play a part.   *The Picture of Dorian Gray.*

One should never make one's *debut* with a scandal. One should reserve that to give an interest to one's old age.

The Picture of Dorian Gray.

*

If a man knows the law there is nothing he cannot do when he likes.

Vera, or The Nihilists.

*

All ways end at the same point . . . Disillusion.

The Picture of Dorian Gray.

XIII

ENGLAND

Wilde had a great affection for the aristocracy of England, whom he envied to a point of snobbishness. He was impressed by the great names of history, the tradition of the Peerage, and in consequence introduced into his plays numerous titled characters. Needless to say the parts in which he imagined himself, were always graced with noble titles.

*

England will never be civilized until she has added Utopia to her dominions.   *The Critic as Artist.*

*

I don't desire to change anything in England except the weather.   *The Picture of Dorian Gray.*

*

England has done one thing; it has invented and established Public Opinion, which is an attempt to organize the ignorance of the community, and to elevate it to the dignity of physical force.   *The Critic as Artist.*

*

The English have a miraculous power of turning wine into water.   *In Conversation.*

*

In England people actually try to be brilliant at breakfast. That is so dreadful of them! Only dull people are brilliant at breakfast.   *An Ideal Husband.*

The English mind is always in a rage. The intellect of the race is wasted on the sordid and stupid quarrels of second-rate politicians and third-rate theologians . . . We are dominated by the fanatic, whose worst vice is his sincerity.

The Critic as Artist.

*

I quite sympathize with the rage of the English democracy against what they call the vices of the upper orders. The masses feel that drunkenness, stupidity, and immorality should be their own special property, and that if any one of us makes an ass of himself he is poaching on their preserves.

The Picture of Dorian Gray.

*

Our countrymen never recognize a description . . . They are more cunning than practical. When they make up their ledger, they balance stupidity by wealth, and vice by hypocrisy.

The Picture of Dorian Gray.

*

. . . Tartuffe has emigrated to England and opened a shop.

The Picture of Dorian Gray.

*

I don't think England should be represented abroad by an unmarried man . . . It might lead to complications.

A Woman of No Importance.

*

MRS. CHEVELEY: . . . a typical Englishman, always dull and usually violent.   *An Ideal Husband.*

*

The Peerage is the one book a young man about town should know thoroughly and it is the best thing in fiction the English have ever done.   *A Woman of No Importance.*

Bosie (Lord Alfred Douglas) has no real enjoyment of a joke unless he thinks there is a good chance of the other person being pained or annoyed. It is an entirely English trait. The English type and symbol of a joke being the jug on the half-opened door, or the distribution of orange peel on the pavement of a crowded thoroughfare. *Letter from Paris, June 1898.*

*

One of those characteristic British faces that, once seen are never remembered. *In Conversation.*

*

Bayswater is a place where people always get lost, and where there are no guides. *In Conversation.*

*

To disagree with three-fourths of the British public on all points is one of the first elements of sanity, one of the deepest consolations in all moments of spiritual doubt.

In Conversation (America).

*

The first time that the absolute stupidity of the English people was ever revealed to me was one Sunday at the Oxford University Church when the preacher opened his sermon in something this way : " When a young man says, not in polished banter but in sober earnestness, that he finds it difficult to live up to the level of his blue china, there has crept into the cloistered shades a form of heathenism which it is our bounden duty to fight against and crush out if possible." I need hardly say that we were delighted and amused at the typical English way in which our ideas were misunderstood. They took our epigrams as earnest, and our parodies as prose. *From a lecture in America.*

*

. . . it is not so easy to be unpractical as the ignorant Philistine imagines. It were well for England if it were so. There is no country in the world so much in need of unpractical people as this country of ours. With us, Thought is degraded by its constant association with practice. *The Critic as Artist.*

120

... the real weakness of England lies, not in incomplete armaments or unfortified coasts, not in the poverty that creeps through sunless lanes, or the drunkenness that brawls in loathsome courts, but simply in the fact that her ideals are emotional and not intellectual.   *The Critic as Artist.*

*

In this country it is enough for a man to have distinction and brains for every common tongue to wag against him.   And what sort of lives do these people who pose as being moral lead themselves.   We are.in the native land of the hypocrite.
                    The Picture of Dorian Gray.

*

West Kensington is a district to which you drive until the horse drops dead, when the cabman gets down to make enquiries.
                    In Conversation.

*

Somehow I don't think I shall live to see the new century—if another century began and I was still alive, it would.really be more than the English could stand.   *In Conversation.*

*

On the British Race:
It represents the survival of the pushing.
                    The Picture of Dorian Gray.

*

The English can't stand a man who is always saying he is right, but they are very fond of a man who admits he has been in the wrong.   *An Ideal Husband.*

*

There is an Italian cook—also the lad Eolo who waits at table. His father said that he was christened Eolo because he was born on a night on which there was a dreadful wind !   I think it is rather nice to have thought of such a name.   An English peasant would probably have said " We called him John, sir, because we were getting in the hay at the time."

                    Letter from Switzerland, February 1899.

XIV

AMERICA

When Oscar Wilde arrived at New York in 1882 he was regarded, and justifiably, as an oddity. His remarks that he had nothing to declare except his genius, and that he was disappointed with the Atlantic gained him more publicity than the theory of aestheticism which he expounded. His lectures amused the Americans and they laughed even louder at the seriousness with which he regarded his mission.

*

On arrival in America:
I am not exactly pleased with the Atlantic, it is not so majestic as I expected.   *In Conversation.*

*

On the return voyage:
The Atlantic has been greatly misunderstood.
                                                            In Conversation

*

We have really everything in common with America nowadays, except, of course, language.   *The Canterville Ghost.*

*

. . . the discovery of America was the beginning of the death of art.   *In Conversation.*

*

When I had to fill in a census paper I gave my age as 19, my profession as genius, my infirmity as talent.   *In Conversation.*

You have heard of me, I fear, through the medium of your somewhat imaginative newspapers as . . . a young man . . . whose greatest difficulty in life was the difficulty of living up to the level of his blue china—a paradox from which England has never recovered. *A Lecture in America.*

*

On being asked by an American theatrical manager to make some changes in " Vera " then being considered for production:
" Who am I to tamper with a masterpiece? "
In Conversation.

*

I am impelled for the first time to breathe a fervent prayer. Save me from my disciples. *A Lecture in America.*

*

Perhaps, after all, America never has been discovered. I myself would say that it had merely been detected.
The Picture of Dorian Gray.

*

On American girls:
Pretty and charming—little oases of pretty unreasonableness in a vast desert of practical common sense. *In Conversation.*

*

It is a popular superstition that a visitor to the more distant parts of the United States is spoken to as " Stranger." But when I went to Texas I was called " Captain "; when I got to the centre of the country I was addressed as " Colonel "; and, on arriving at the borders of Mexico as " General."
In Conversation (America).

*

In America life is one long expectoration. *In Conversation.*

*

The Americans are certainly great hero-worshippers, and always take heroes from the criminal classes. *Letter.*

LADY CAROLINE : . . . These American girls carry off all the good matches. Why can't they stay in their own country? They are always telling us it is the Paradise of Women.

LORD ILLINGWORTH : It is, Lady Caroline. That is why, like Eve, they are so extremely anxious to get out of it.

A Woman of No Importance.

*

Many American ladies on leaving their native land adopt an appearance of chronic ill-health, under the impression that it is a form of European refinement. *The Canterville Ghost.*

*

Among the more elderly inhabitants of the South I found a melancholy tendency to date every event of importance on the late War. " How beautiful the moon is tonight," I once remarked to a gentleman standing near me. " Yes," was his reply, " but you should have seen it before the War."

In Conversation (America).

*

American Men:

I can stand brute force but brute reason is quite unbearable. There is something unfair about its use. It is like hitting below the intellect. *In Conversation.*

*

It is the noisiest country that ever existed. Such continual turmoil must ultimately be destruction of the musical faculty.

In Conversation.

*

I would rather have discovered Mrs. Langtry than have discovered America. *In Conversation.*

*

The crude commercialism of America, its materialism spirit, its indifference to the poetical side of things, and its lack of imagination and of high unattainable ideas, are entirely due to that country having adopted for its national hero a man who, according to his own confession, was incapable of telling a lie, and it is not too much to say that the story of George Washington and the cherry-tree has done more harm, and in a shorter space of time than any other moral tale in the whole of literature—and the amusing part of the whole thing is that the story of the cherry-tree is an absolute myth.   *The Decay of Lying.*

*

I believe a most serious problem for the American people to consider is the cultivation of better manners. It is the most noticeable, the most principal, defect in American civilization.

In Conversation (America).

*

There are no trappings, no pageantry, and no gorgeous ceremonies. I saw only two processions : one was the Fire Brigade preceded by the Police, the other was the Police preceded by the Fire Brigade.   *In Conversation (America).*

*

Washington has too many bronze generals.

In Conversation (America).

*

America reminds me of one of Edgar Allan Poe's exquisite poems, because it is full of belles.

In Conversation (America).

*

In all my journeys through the country, the very well-dressed men that I saw were the Western miners. As I looked at them I could not help thinking with regret of the time when these picturesque miners would have made their fortunes and would go East to assume again all the abominations of modern fashionable attire. Indeed, so concerned was I that I made some of them promise that when they again appeared on the more crowded scenes of Eastern civilization they would still continue to wear their lovely costume. But I do not believe they will.

In Conversation (America).

125

Let the Greek carve his lions and the Goth his dragons:
buffalo and wild deer are the animals for you.

A Lecture in America.

*

The youth of America is their oldest tradition. It has been
going on now for three hundred years. To hear them talk we
would imagine they were in their first childhood. As far as
civilization goes they are in their second.

A Woman of No Importance.

*

The gold is ready for you in unexhausted treasure, stored up
in the mountain hollow or strewn on the river sand, and was not
given to you merely for barren speculation. There should be
some better record of it left in your history than the merchant's
panic and the ruined home.   *A Lecture in America.*

*

All Americans lecture . . . I suppose it is something in their
climate.   *A Woman of No Importance.*

*

LADY CAROLINE: There are a great many things you haven't
got in America, I am told, Miss Worsley. They say you have no
ruins, and no curiosities.

MRS. ALLONBY: . . . What nonsense! They have their mothers
and their manners.

HESTER: The English aristocracy supply us with our curiosities.

LADY CAROLINE: They are sent over to us every summer,
regularly, in the steamers, and propose to us the day after they
land. As for ruins, we are trying to build up something that will
last longer than brick or stone.

LADY HUNSTANTON: What is that, dear? Ah, yes, an Iron
Exhibition, is it not, at that place that has the curious name?

A Woman of No Importance.

" They say that when good Americans die they go to Paris,"
chuckled Sir Thomas . . .

" Really! and where do bad Americans go to when they die? "
inquired the Duchess.

" They go to America," murmured Lord Henry.

The Picture of Dorian Gray.

＊

Oscar Wilde referred to the Niagara Falls as—" simply a vast
unnecessary amount of water going the wrong way and then
falling over unnecessary rocks."

" But at least you'll admit they are wonderful waterfalls? "
he was asked.

" The wonder would be if the water did not fall! Every
American bride is taken there and the sight of the stupendous
waterfall must be one of the earliest, if not the keenest, disappoint-
ments in American married life."

In Conversation (America).

XV

JOURNALISM

The English Press parodied and jeered at the person of Oscar Wilde, although the caricatures which appeared in Punch served as useful publicity. Without malice himself he was never able to understand the insults and sneers of the journalists of his day.

*

Journalism justifies its own existence by the great Darwinian principle of the survival of the vulgarest.   *In Conversation.*

*

VICOMTE DE NANJAC :   I read all your English newspapers. I find them so amusing.
LORD GORING : Then, my dear Nanjac, you must certainly read between the lines.   *An Ideal Husband.*

*

The newspapers chronicle with degrading avidity the sins of the second-rate, and with the conscientiousness of the illiterate give us accurate and prosaic details of the doings of people of absolutely no interest whatever.   *In Conversation.*

*

Modern journalism, by giving us the opinions of the un-educated, keeps us in touch with the ignorance of the community.
    The Critic as Artist.

*

With regard to modern journalists, they always apologize to one in private for what they have written against one in public.
    The Soul of Man Under Socialism.

In the old days men had the rack, now they have the Press.
The Soul of Man Under Socialism.

*

Journalism is unreadable, and literature is not read.
The Critic as Artist.

*

The public have an insatiable curiosity to know everything, except what is worth knowing. Journalism, conscious of this, and having tradesman-like habits, supplies their demands. In centuries before ours the public nailed the ears of journalists to the pump. That was quite hideous. In this century journalists have nailed their own ears to the keyhole.
The Soul of Man Under Socialism.

*

To have a style so gorgeous that it conceals the subject is one of the highest achievements of an important and much admired school of Fleet Street leader-writers.   *Pen, Pencil and Poison.*

*

Instead of monopolizing the seat of judgment, journalism should be apologizing in the dock.   *In Conversation.*

*

Leader writers:
Who are these scribes who, passing with purposeless alacrity from the *Police News* to the Parthenon, and from crime to criticism, sway with such serene incapacity the office which they have so lately swept?
In Correspondence (with Joaquin Miller).

*

What is behind the leading article but prejudice, stupidity, cant and twaddle?   *In Conversation.*

Somebody—was it Burke?—called journalism the fourth estate. That was true at the time, no doubt. But at the present moment it really is the only estate. It has eaten up the other three. The Lords Temporal say nothing, the Lords Spiritual have nothing to say, and the House of Commons has nothing to say and says it. We are dominated by Journalism. In America the President reigns for four years, and Journalism goes on for ever and ever. *The Soul of Man Under Socialism.*

*

The journalist is always reminding the public of the existence of the artist. That is unnecessary of him. He is always reminding the artist of the existence of the public. That is indecent of him . . . Journalists record only what happens. What does it matter what happens? It is only the abiding things that are interesting, not the horrid incidents of everyday life. Creation for the joy of creation is the aim of the artist, and that is why the artist is a more divine type than the saint.
In an Interview.

*

Every time my name is mentioned in a paper I write at once to admit that I am the Messiah. Why is Pears' soap successful? Not because it is better or cheaper than any other soap, but because it is more strenuously puffed. The Journalist is my " John the Baptist." *In Conversation.*

*

Newspapers even have degenerated. They may now be absolutely relied upon. One feels it as one wades through their columns. It is always the unreadable that occurs.
The Decay of Lying.

*

MRS. CHEVELEY : . . . I am quite looking forward to meeting your clever husband, Lady Chiltern . . . They actually succeed in spelling his name right in the newspapers. That in itself is fame, on the Continent. *An Ideal Husband.*

In France, in fact, they limit the journalist, and allow the artist almost perfect freedom. Here we allow absolute freedom to the journalist, and entirely limit the artist.

The Soul of Man Under Socialism.

*

At present the newspapers are trying hard to induce the public to judge a sculptor, for instance, never by his statues but by the way he treats his wife; a painter by the amount of his income; and a poet by the colour of his necktie.   *A Lecture.*

*

Lying for the sake of a monthly salary is, of course, well known in Fleet Street, and the profession of a political leader-writer is not without advantages. But it is said to be a somewhat dull occupation, and it certainly does not lead to much beyond a kind of ostentatious obscurity.   *The Decay of Lying.*

*

It was a fatal day when the public discovered that the pen is mightier than the paving stone, and can be made as offensive as the brickbat. They at once sought for the journalist, found him, developed him, and made him their industrious and well-paid servant.   *The Soul of Man Under Socialism.*

XVI

POLITICS

Wilde was recognized in political circles as a brilliant talker despite the many derogatory references he made to the manner in which politicians conducted their affairs.

*

KELVIL: May I ask, Lord Illingworth, if you regard the House of Lords as a better institution than the House of Commons?
LORD ILLINGWORTH: A much better institution of course. We in the House of Lords are never in touch with public opinion. That makes us a civilized body.   *A Woman of No Importance.*

*

In England a man who can't talk morality twice a week to a large, popular, immoral audience is quite over as a serious politician.   *An Ideal Husband.*

*

He thinks like a Tory, and talks like a Radical, and that's so important nowadays.   *Lady Windermere's Fan.*

*

There is hardly a single person in the House of Commons worth painting; though many of them would be better for a little whitewashing.   *The Picture of Dorian Gray.*

*

Wherever there is a man who exercises authority, there is a man who resists authority!   *The Soul of Man Under Socialism.*

MABEL CHILTERN: Oh! I hope you are not going to leave me all alone with Lord Goring? Especially at such an early hour in the day.

LORD CAVERSHAM: I am afraid I can't take him with me to Downing Street. It is not the Prime Minister's day for seeing the unemployed.   *An Ideal Husband.*

*

If Socialism is Authoritarian; if there are Governments armed with economic power as they are now with political power; if, in a word, we are to have Industrial Tyrannies, then the last state of man will be worse than the first.
                              The Soul of Man Under Socialism.

*

We are trying at the present time to stave off the coming crisis, the coming revolution as my friends the Fabianists call it, by means of doles and alms. Well when the revolution or crisis arrives, we shall be powerless because we shall know nothing.
                              The Critic as Artist.

*

What we want are unpractical people who see beyond the moment and think beyond the day. Those who try to lead the people can only do so by following the mob. It is through the voice crying in the wilderness that the ways of the gods must be prepared.   *The Critic as Artist.*

*

Nothing is impossible in Russia but reform.
                              Vera, or The Nihilists.

*

. . . what is a practical scheme? A practical scheme is either one that is already in existence, or a scheme that could be carried out under existing conditions. But it is exactly existing conditions that one objects to; and any scheme that could accept these conditions is wrong and foolish. The conditions will be done away with, and human nature will change. The only thing that

133

one really knows about human nature is that it changes . . . The error of Louis the XIV was that he thought human nature would always be the same. The result of his error was the French Revolution. *The Soul of Man Under Socialism.*

*

Picturesqueness cannot survive the House of Commons.
An Ideal Husband.

*

High hopes were once formed of democracy; but democracy means simply the bludgeoning of the people by the people for the people. *The Soul of Man Under Socialism.*

*

There is this to be said in favour of the despot, that he, being an individual, may have culture, while the mob, being a monster, has none. One who is an Emperor and King may stoop to pick up a brush for a painter, but when democracy stoops down it is merely to throw mud. And yet the democracy have not so far to stoop as the emperor. In fact, if they want to throw mud they have not to stoop at all. But there is no necessity to separate the monarch from the mob; all authority is equally bad. There are three kinds of despots. There is the despot who tyrannizes over the body. There is the despot who tyrannizes over the soul. There is the despot who tyrannizes over the soul and body alike. The first is called the Prince. The second is called the Pope. The third is called the People. *The Soul of Man Under Socialism.*

*

People sometimes enquire what form of government it is most suitable for an artist to live under. To this question there is only one answer. The form of government that is most suitable to the artist is no government at all. *The Soul of Man Under Socialism.*

Patriotism is the virtue of the vicious.   *In Conversation.*

*

Agitators are a set of interfering meddling people, who come down to some perfectly contented class of the community and sow the seeds of discontent amongst them.   That is the reason why agitators are so absolutely necessary.

The Soul of Man Under Socialism.

*

It is to be regretted that a portion of our community should be practically in slavery, but to propose to solve the problem by enslaving the entire community is childish.

The Soul of Man Under Socialism.

*

It is immoral to use private property in order to alleviate the horrible evils that result from the institution of private property. It is both immoral and unfair.

The Soul of Man Under Socialism.

*

Good Kings are the only dangerous enemies that modern democracy has.   *Vera, or The Nihilists.*

*

Socialism annihilates family life, for instance.   With the abolition of private property, marriage in its present form must disappear.   *The Soul of Man Under Socialism..*

*

A Russian who lives happily under the present system of government in Russia must either believe that man has no soul, or that, if he has, it is not worth developing.

The Soul of Man Under Socialism.

*

Only people who look dull ever get into the House of Commons, and only people who are dull ever succeed there.

An Ideal Husband.

He pretends to be devoted to the people, and lives in a palace; preaches socialism, and draws a salary that would support a province. *Vera, or The Nihilists.*

*

What a Communist he is! He would have an equal distribution of sin as well as property. *Vera, or The Nihilists.*

*

While to the claims of charity a man may yield and yet be free, to the claims of conformity no man may yield and remain free at all. *The Soul of Man Under Socialism.*

*

All authority is quite degrading. It degrades those who exercise it, and it degrades those over whom it is exercised.
The Soul of Man Under Socialism.

*

Whenever a community . . . or a government of any kind, attempts to dictate to the artist what he is to do, art either entirely vanishes, or becomes stereotyped, or degenerates into a low and ignoble form of craft!
The Soul of Man Under Socialism.

*

In a community like ours, where property confers immense distinction, social position, honour, respect, titles, and other pleasant things of the kind, man being naturally ambitious, makes it his aim to accumulate this property, and goes on wearily and tediously accumulating it long after he has got more than he wants, or can use, or enjoy, or perhaps even know of. Man will kill himself by overwork in order to secure property, and really, considering the enormous advantages that property brings, one is hardly surprised.
The Soul of Man Under Socialism.

*

As long as war is regarded as wicked, it will always have its fascination. When it is looked upon as vulgar it will cease to be popular. *The Critic as Artist.*

XVII

APPEARANCES

He was extravagant in dress and regarded the ornate façade which he presented to the world as being almost as important as the things he said. In his early days in London he wore a velvet beret, lace shirts, velveteen knee-breeches and black silk stockings. Later he adopted the conventional attire of the day, but always he was meticulous and dandified in his dress.

*

It is only the shallow people who do not judge by appearances.
The Picture of Dorian Gray.

*

He atones for being occasionally somewhat over-dressed, by being always absolutely over-educated.
The Picture of Dorian Gray.

*

With an evening coat and a white tie, anybody, even a stock-broker, can gain a reputation for being civilized.
The Picture of Dorian Gray.

*

A really well-made buttonhole is the only link between Art and Nature.
Phrases and Philosophies for the Use of the Young.

*

One should either be a work of art, or wear a work of art.
Phrases and Philosophies for the Use of the Young.

137

Wilde claimed that he once saw in a French journal, under a drawing of a bonnet, the words:
" With this style the mouth is worn slightly open."

In Conversation.

*

He has nothing, but looks everything. What more can one desire? *The Importance of Being Earnest.*

*

A well-tied tie is the first serious step in life.

The Importance of Being Earnest.

*

She wore far too much rouge last night and not quite enough clothes. That is always a sign of despair in a woman.

An Ideal Husband.

*

Fashion is what one wears oneself. What is unfashionable is what other people wear. *An Ideal Husband.*

*

Knaves nowadays do look so honest that honest folk are forced to look like knaves so as to be different.

The Duchess of Padua.

*

In matters of grave importance, style, not sincerity, is the vital thing. *The Importance of Being Earnest.*

*

A mask tells us more than a face. *Pen, Pencil and Poison.*

*

LORD GORING : . . . I should fancy Mrs. Cheveley is one of those very modern women of our time who find a new scandal as becoming as a new bonnet, and air them both in the Park every afternoon at five-thirty. *An Ideal Husband.*

Do you believe that the Athenian women were like the stately dignified figures of the Parthenon frieze, or like those marvellous goddesses who sat in the triangular pediments of the same building? If you judge from the art, they certainly were so. But read an authority like Aristophanes, for instance. You will find that the Athenian ladies laced tightly, wore high-heeled shoes, dyed their hair yellow, painted and rouged their faces and were exactly like any silly fashionable or fallen creatures of our own day. The fact is that we look back on the ages entirely through the medium of art, and art, very fortunately, has never once told us the truth. *The Decay of Lying.*

*

One should never give a woman anything she can't wear in the evening. *An Ideal Husband.*

*

Second Citizen:
These great folk have not much sense, so Providence makes it up to them in fine clothes. *The Duchess of Padua.*

*

What a pity it is that Luther knew nothing of dress, had no sense of the becoming. He had courage but no fineness of perception. I'm afraid his neckties would always have been quite shocking. *In Conversation.*

*

Cavaliers and Puritans are interesting for their costumes and not for their convictions. *In Conversation.*

*

A man is called affected, nowadays, if he dresses as he likes to dress. But in doing that he is acting in a perfectly natural manner. *The Soul of Man under Socialism.*

*

When she is in a very smart gown, she looks like an *edition de luxe* of a wicked French novel meant specially for the English market. *In Conversation.*

139

To see the frock-coat of the drawing room done in bronze, or the double waistcoat perpetuated in marble, adds a new horror to death. *In Conversation (America).*

✳

Greek dress was in its essence inartistic. Nothing should reveal the body but the body.

Phrases and Philosophies for the Use of the Young.

XVIII

CONVERSATION

To the acclaim of Wilde's greatness and genius as a conversationalist there is not one dissenting voice, or record, from amongst those who heard him speak. The evidence in his favour is overwhelming yet there are still a few, who have come later, who cavil and suggest that his conversational powers are exaggerated; that his witticisms were diligently prepared and studiously rehearsed beforehand. No doubt, he often used appropriate remarks from the store of his memory whenever the occasion suited, who would not? But it is just as reasonable to deduce that these same remarks were spontaneously born in the first place. During his trial the initiative obviously did not rest with Wilde and yet the facility of his unrehearsed repartee was quite as brilliant as the many examples of his recorded impromptu remarks.

Wilde lived and thought amid a welter of words and fluency in speech was as natural to him as breathing. The wit, which he employed so often, was prompted by the great sense of humour which governed his whole attitude to life.

It has even been suggested that Wilde lacked a sense of humour; the one quality which is more evident than any other in a survey of his works and conversation. A sense of humour is something that one must possess to be able to recognize the presence, or the absence of it, in others, and Wilde was as quick to appreciate humour in others as he was to reel off a sententious and witty reply.

He was a fantastic, grotesque, posturing figure, amused to amuse the world. With his solemn dignity which lent greater humour to his remarks, he was Cynicism wearing a false nose; Decorum standing on its head to be noticed.

141

Criticize his morals, his life, his works; yes, of course. But never doubt his greatness as an unexcelled conversationalist.

Robert Louis Stevenson wrote "The first duty of man is to speak: that is his chief business in the world" Oscar Wilde certainly made it his.

*

There is only one thing in the world worse than being talked about, and that is not being talked about.

The Picture or Dorian Gray.

*

I may have said the same thing before . . . But my explanation, I am sure, will always be different.   *In Conversation.*

*

MRS. ALLONBY : . . . you should certainly know Ernest, Lady Stutfield. It is only fair to tell you beforehand he has got no conversation at all.

LADY STUTFIELD : I adore silent men.

MRS. ALLONBY : Oh, Ernest isn't silent. He talks the whole time. But he has got no conversation.

A Woman of No Importance.

*

Murder is always a mistake . . . One should never do anything that one cannot talk about after dinner.

The Picture of Dorian Gray.

*

I love scandals about other people, but scandals about myself don't interest me. They have not got the charm of novelty.

The Picture of Dorian Gray.

*

Between me and life there is a mist of words always. I throw probability out of the window for the sake of a phrase, and the chance of an epigram makes me desert truth. Still I do aim at making a work of art.   *In Conversation.*

The value of the telephone is the value of what two people have to say. *In Conversation.*

*

" There is no good talking to him," said a Dragonfly, who was sitting on the top of a large brown bulrush; " no good at all, for he has gone away."

" Well, that is his loss, not mine," answered the Rocket. " I am not going to stop talking to him merely because he pays no attention. I like hearing myself talk. It is one of my greatest pleasures. I often have long conversations all by myself, and I am so clever that sometimes I don't understand a single word of what I am saying." *The Remarkable Rocket.*

*

LORD CAVERSHAM : Do you always really understand what you say sir?
LORD GORING (*after some hesitation*): Yes, father, if I listen attentively. *An Ideal Husband.*

*

I dislike arguments of any kind. They are always vulgar, and often convincing. *The Importance of Being Earnest.*

*

Nowadays to be intelligible is to be found out.
Lady Windermere's Fan.

*

PRINCE PAUL : . . . I find these Cabinet Councils extremely tiring.
PRINCE PETROVITCH : Naturally, you are always speaking.
PRINCE PAUL : No; I think it must be that I have to listen sometimes. It is so exhausting not to talk.
Vera, or The Nihilists.

*

LORD GORING : . . . I usually say what I really think. A great mistake nowadays. It makes one so liable to be misunderstood.
An Ideal Husband.

143

I don't at all like knowing what people say of me behind my back. It makes one far too conceited. *An Ideal Husband.*

*

Everything you have said to-day seems to me excessively immoral. It has been most interesting, listening to you.
A Woman of No Importance.

*

Gossip is charming! . . . History is merely gossip. But scandal is gossip made tedious by morality.
Lady Windermere's Fan.

*

Every good storyteller nowadays starts with the end, and then goes on to the beginning, and concludes with the middle. That is the new method. *The Devoted Friend.*

*

A man who can dominate a London dinner-table can dominate the world. The future belongs to the dandy. It is the exquisites who are going to rule. *A Woman of No Importance.*

*

I like to do all the talking myself. It saves time and prevents arguments. *The Remarkable Rocket.*

*

That some change will take place before this century has drawn to its close we have no doubt whatsoever. Bored by the tedious and improving conversation of those who have neither the wit to exaggerate nor the genius to romance, tired of the intelligent person whose reminiscences are always based on memory, whose statements are invariably limited by probability, and who is at any time liable to be corroborated by the merest Philistine who happens to be present, Society sooner or later must return to its lost leader, the cultured and fascinating liar.
The Decay of Lying.

Lots of people act well but very few people talk well, which shows that talking is much more the difficult thing of the two, and much the finer thing also. *The Devoted Friend.*

*

I like talking to a brick wall, it's the only thing in the world that never contradicts me. *Lady Windermere's Fan.*

*

There are things that are right to say, but that may be said at the wrong time and to the wrong people.
A Woman of No Importance.

*

I am afraid you have been listening to the conversation of someone older than yourself. That is always a dangerous thing to do, and if you allow it to degenerate into a habit you will find it absolutely fatal to any intellectual development.
The Critic as Artist.

*

Conversation should touch everything but should concentrate itself on nothing. *The Critic as Artist.*

*

Arguments are extremely vulgar, for everybody in good society holds exactly the same opinions.
The Remarkable Rocket.

*

Learned conversation is either the affectation of the ignorant or the profession of the mentally unemployed. And as for what is called improving conversation, that is merely the foolish method by which the still more foolish philanthropist feebly tries to disarm the just rancour of the criminal classes. *The Critic as Artist.*

*

Questions are never indiscreet. Answers sometimes are.
An Ideal Husband.

145

I hate people who talk about themselves, as you do, when one wants to talk about oneself, as I do.   *The Remarkable Rocket.*

*

A man who allows himself to be convinced by an argument is a thoroughly unreasonable person.   *An Ideal Husband.*

*

DORIAN GRAY: You would sacrifice anybody, Harry, for the sake of an epigram.   *The Picture of Dorian Gray.*

*

The clever people never listen, and the stupid people never talk.   *The Woman of No Importance.*

*

It is much more difficult to talk about a thing than to do it. In the sphere of actual life that is of course obvious.   Anybody can make history.   Only a great man can write it.
The Critic as Artist.

*

I would much sooner talk scandal in a drawing-room than treason in a cellar.   *Vera, or The Nihilists.*

*

She doesn't care much for eloquence in others.   She thinks it a little loud.   *An Ideal Husband.*

*

One dagger will do more than a hundred epigrams.
Vera, or The Nihilists.

*

It is always worth while asking a question, though it is not always worth while answering one.   *An Ideal Husband.*

*

The only reason, indeed, that excuses one for asking any question is simple curiosity.   *The Picture of Dorian Gray.*

He never said a brilliant or even an ill-natured thing in his life.   *The Model Millionaire.*

*

When people talk to us about others they are usually dull. When they talk to us about themselves they are nearly always interesting, and if one could shut them up, when they become wearisome, as easily as one can shut up a book of which one has grown wearied, they would be perfect absolutely.
                                                                                     The Critic as Artist.

*

It is only the intellectually lost who can argue.
                                                                        The Picture of Dorian Gray.

*

I can't listen to anyone unless he attracts me by a charming style or by beauty of theme.   *In Conversation.*

*

Oh, I'm so glad you've come.   There are a hundred things I want not to say to you.   *In Conversation.*

*

The well-bred contradict other people.   The wise contradict themselves.   *Phrases and Philosophies for the Use of the Young.*

*

It is perfectly monstrous the way people go about nowadays saying things against one behind one's back that are absolutely and entirely true.   *The Picture of Dorian Gray.*

*

When people agree with me I always feel that I must be wrong.
                                                                                     The Critic as Artist.

147

There is no mode of action, no form of emotion, that we do not share with the lower animals. It is only by language that we rise above them—by language, which is the parent not the child of thought. *In Conversation.*

*

After all, the only proper intoxication is conversation.

Letter from Paris, May 1898.

XIX

CONVERSATION PIECES

It may be mistakenly misconstrued from this collection of sayings' that Wilde's conversation mainly consisted of brilliant epigrams and witty comments. This, of course, is not so, for his witticisms were the decorations which embroidered his discourses, and the salient feature of his conversation was the facility with which he invented stories to illustrate a particular point.

Included in this chapter is the story of a magnet, as told originally to Richard Le Gallienne. Wilde improvised this story to illustrate Free Will as an illusion and Destiny as inescapable.

His talk abounded with such stories and although many are recorded, as remembered, by his biographers, regrettably very few exist in Wilde's own words. The most representative example from his works is " Lord Arthur Savile's Crime " and even this is inferior to the much shorter original which was told to Graham Robertson.

A typical improvisation, in which Wilde was illustrating the value of presence of mind in an emergency, is recorded by E. F. Benson in his autobiography and by Hesketh Pearson in his admirable book " The Life of Oscar Wilde " (surely the definitive biography). The following is merely a brief resumé, unfortunately not in Wilde's words, to demonstrate the applicability of his extemporizations.

The story concerns a well-known actor, who is alive only by reason of his daring coolness and exemplary presence of mind when faced with terrible danger. He was playing the lead in a successful play to crowded houses at a lesser-known theatre. One evening, at a particularly dramatic period in the performance, when the audience were engrossed in the action of the play, clouds of smoke bellowed forth from the wings and devouring tongues of flame licked hungrily at the curtains and scenery.

The audience were horrified as they watched the flames sweep rapidly and remorselessly, like a forest fire, across the stage. Until, in one dreadful moment they realized the enormity and danger of the situation, and then, in a terrific panic they rose from their seats and frantically stampeded towards the exits. Immediately, the whole auditorium became a seething mass of frenzied bodies, striving and tearing at each other.

The well-known actor realizing the desperate situation, saw that there was a tremendous danger that many would be trampled underfoot and indeed, that unless action was taken at once very few would escape alive. With remarkable and commendable presence of mind he leapt on to the stage, and then, standing with statuesque calm, arms outstretched, his voice rang out, clarion-clear, above the tumult.

The terror-stricken, unruly audience, recognizing the well-known resonant tones were calmed by the coolness, and re-assured by the voice, of the actor. Speaking with perfect composure, he explained that the fire was safely under control and that the only danger was the liability of injuries that would be caused by their own wild panic. The audience, fears dispelled, at his bidding quietly resumed their seats, feeling somewhat ashamed of their hysteria.

When all was calm and the orderly pattern restored, the well-known actor leapt nimbly from the stage and vanished through the nearest exit.

At that very moment, and whilst the audience were still mystified, the auditorium suddenly filled with black, choking smoke, whilst with an angry, terrifying roar the flames leapt and crackled as their hot breath enveloped the entire theatre. Alas, it was too late and not a soul escaped; except of course, the actor, who by his admirable presence of mind, was the first and only person to leave the doomed building alive.

The following examples cannot possibly do justice to Wilde's excellence as a raconteur and are merely intended to indicate the character of this integral part of his conversation.

*

Once upon a time there was a magnet, and in its close neighbourhood were some steel filings. One day two or three

150

little filings felt a sudden desire to go and visit the magnet, and they began to talk of what a pleasant thing it would be to do. Other filings nearby overheard their conversation, and they, too, became infected with the same desire. Still others joined them, till at last all the filings began to discuss the matter, and more and more their vague desire grew into an impulse.

"Why not go to-day?" said some of them; but others were of opinion that it would be better to wait till to-morrow. Meanwhile, without their having noticed it, they had been involuntarily moving nearer to the magnet, which lay there quite still, apparently taking no heed of them. And so they went on discussing all the time insensibly drawing nearer to their neighbour; and the more they talked, the more they felt the impulse growing stronger, till the more impatient ones declared that they would go that day, whatever the rest did. Some were heard to say that it was their duty to visit the magnet, and that they ought to have gone long ago. And while they talked, they moved nearer and nearer, without realizing that they had moved. Then, at last, the impatient ones prevailed, and, with one irresistible impulse, the whole body cried out, "There is no use waiting, we will go to-day. We will go now. We will go at once." And then in one unanimous mass they swept along, and in another moment were clinging fast to the magnet on every side. Then the magnet smiled—for the steel filings had no doubt at all but that they were paying that visit of their own free will

From Richard Le Gallienne's " The Romantic 90s." (Putnam).

*

The Disciple:
When Narcissus· died the pool of his pleasure changed from a cup of sweet waters into a cup of salt tears, and the Oreads came weeping through the woodland that they might sing to the pool and give it comfort.

And when they saw the pool had changed from a cup of sweet waters into a cup of salt tears, they loosened the green tresses of their hair and cried to the pool and said, " We do not wonder that you should mourn in this manner for Narcissus, so beautiful was he."

" But was Narcissus beautiful? " said the pool.

" Who should know better than you? " answered the Oreads.
" Us he did ever pass by, but you he sought for, and would
lie on your banks and look down at you, and in the mirror of
your waters he would mirror his own beauty "

And the pool answered, " But I loved Narcissus because, as he
lay on my banks and looked down at me, in the mirror of his
eyes I saw ever my own beauty mirrored."   *Poems in Prose.*

*

I was telling them (his two sons) stories last night of little boys
who were naughty and made their mother cry, and what
dreadful things would happen to them unless they became better;
and what do you think one of them answered?   He asked me
what punishment could be reserved for naughty papas, who did
not come home till the early morning, and made their mother
cry far more!   *In Conversation.*

*

Shortly after Mr. Stevenson published his curious psychological
study of transformation, a friend of mine, called Mr. Hyde, who
was in the north of London, and being anxious to get to a railway
station, took what he thought would be a short cut, lost his way,
and found himself in a network of mean, evil-looking streets.
Feeling rather nervous he began to walk extremely fast, when
suddenly out of an archway ran a child right between his legs.
It fell on the pavement, he tripped over it, and trampled upon it.
Being, of course, very much frightened and a little hurt, it began
to scream, and in a few seconds the whole street was full of rough
people who came pouring out of the houses like ants.   They
surrounded him and asked him his name.   He was just
about to give it when he remembered the opening incident in
Mr. Stevenson's story.   He was so filled with horror at having
realized in his own person that terrible and well-written scene,
and at having done accidentally though in fact, what the
Mr. Hyde of fiction had done with deliberate intent, that he ran
away as hard as he could go.   He was, however, very closely
followed, and finally he took refuge in a surgery, the door of which

happened to be open, where he explained to a young assistant who happened to be there, exactly what had occurred. The humanitarian crowd were induced to go away on his giving them a small sum of money, and as soon as the coast was clear he left; as he passed out, the name on the brass door-plate of the surgery caught his eye. It was " Jekyll." At least it should have been.

The Decay of Lying.

*

It is the duty of every father to write fairy-tales for his children, but the mind of a child is a great mystery. It is incalculable, and who shall divine it, or bring to it its own peculiar delights? You humbly spread before it the treasures of your imagination, and they are as dross. For example, a day or two ago Cyril came to me with the question, " Father, do you ever dream? " " Why, of course, my darling." It is the first duty of a gentleman to dream." " And what do you dream of? " asked Cyril with a child's disgusting appetite for facts. Then I, believing of course that something picturesque would be expected of me, spoke of magnificent things. " What do I dream of? Oh, I dream of dragons with gold and silver scales, and scarlet flames coming out of their mouths, of eagles with eyes made of diamonds that can see over the whole world at once, of lions with yellow manes and voices like thunder, of elephants with little houses on their backs and tigers and zebras with barred and spotted coats . . . " So I laboured on with my fancy, till observing that Cyril was entirely unimpressed, and indeed quite undisguisedly bored, I came to a humiliating stop, and, turning to him, I said : " But tell me, what do you dream of, Cyril? " His answer was like a divine revelation. " I dream of *pigs*," he said.

From Richard Le Gallienne's " The Romantic 90's." (Putnam).

*

The Master:

Now when the darkness came over the earth Joseph of Arimathea having lighted a torch of pinewood, passed down from the hill into the valley. For he had business in his own home. And kneeling on the flint stones of the Valley of Desolation he saw a young man who was naked and weeping. His hair was

153

the colour of honey, and his body was as a white flower, but he had wounded his body with thorns and on his hair he had set ashes and a crown.

And he who had great possessions said to the young man who was naked and weeping, "I do not wonder that your sorrow is so great, for surely He was a just man."

And the young man answered, " It is not for Him that I am weeping, but for myself. I too have changed water into wine, and I have healed the leper and given sight to the blind. I have walked upon the waters, and from the dwellers in the tombs I have cast out devils. I have fed the hungry in the desert where there was no food, and I have raised the dead from their narrow houses, and at my bidding, and before a great multitude of people, a barren fig-tree withered away. All things this man has done I have done also. And yet they have not crucified me."

Poems in Prose.

*

The Doer of Good:

It was night time and He was alone.

And He saw afar-off the walls of a round city and went towards the city. And when he came near He heard within the city the tread of the feet of joy, and the laughter of the mouth of gladness and the loud noise of many lutes. And He knocked at the gate and certain of the gatekeepers opened it to Him.

And He beheld a house that was of marble and had fair pillars of marble before it. The pillars were hung with garlands, and within and without there were torches of cedar. And He entered the house.

And when He had passed through the hall of the chalcedony and the hall of jasper, and had reached the long hall of feasting, He saw lying on a couch of sea-purple one whose hair was crowned with red roses and whose lips were red with wine. And He went behind him and touched him on the shoulder and said to him, "Why do you live like this?"

And the young man turned round and recognized Him, and made answer and said, "But I was a leper once, and you healed me. How else should I live?"

And He passed out of the house and went again into the street.

After a little while He saw one whose face and raiment were painted and whose feet were shod with pearls. And behind her came, slowly as a hunter, a young man who wore a cloak of two colours. Now the face of the woman was as the fair face of an idol, and the eyes of the young man were bright with lust.

And He followed swiftly and touched the hand of the young man and said to him, "Why do you look at this woman and in such wise?"

And the young man turned round and recognized Him and said, "But I was blind once, and you gave me sight. At what else should I look?" And He ran forward and touched the painted raiment of the woman and said to her, "Is there no way in which to walk save the way of sin?" And the woman turned round and recognized Him, and laughed and said, " But you forgave me my sins, and the way is a pleasant way."

And He passed out of the city.

And when He had passed out of the city He saw seated by the roadside a young man who was weeping.

And He went towards him and touched the long locks of his hair and said to him, " Why are you weeping? "

And the young man looked up and recognized Him and made answer, " But I was dead once and you raised me from the dead, what else should I do but weep?"   *Poems in Prose.*

*

The House of Judgment:

And there was silence in the House of Judgment, and the Man came naked before God.

And God opened the book of the life of the Man.

And God said to the Man, " Thy life has been évil, and thou hast shown cruelty to those who were in need of succour, and to those who lacked help thou hast been bitter and hard of heart. The poor called to thee and thou didst not hearken, and thine eyes were closed to the cry of My afflicted. The inheritance of the fatherless thou didst take unto thyself, and thou didst send foxes into the vineyards of thy neighbour's field. Thou didst take the bread of the children and gave it to the dogs to eat, and My lepers who lived in the marshes, and were at peace and praised me thou didst drive forth onto the highways, and out of My earth out of which I made thee thou didst spill innocent blood."

And the Man made answer and said, " Even so did I."

And again God opened the book of the life of the Man.

And God said to the Man, " Thy life hath been evil, and the beauty I have shown thou hast sought for, and the Good I have hidden thou didst pass by. The walls of thy chamber were painted with images, and from the bed of thy abominations thou didst rise up to the sound of flutes. Thou didst build seven altars to the sins I have suffered, and didst eat of the thing that may not be eaten, and the purple of thy raiment was broidered with the three signs of shame. Thine idols were neither of Gold nor of silver that endure, but of flesh which dieth. Thou didst stain their hair with perfumes and put pomegranates in their hands. Thou didst stain their feet with saffron and spread carpets before them. With antimony thou didst stain their eyelids and their bodies thou didst smear with myrrh. Thou didst bow thyself to the ground before them, and the thrones of thine idols were set in the sun. Thou didst show to the sun thy shame and to the moon thy madness."

And the Man answered and said, " Even so did I."

And a third time God opened the book of the life of the Man. And God said to the Man, " Evil hath been thy life, and with evil didst thou requite good, and with wrongdoing kindness, the hands that fed thee thou didst wound, and the breasts that gave thee suck thou didst despise. He who came to thee with water went away thirsting, and the outlawed men who hid thee in their tents at night thou didest betray before dawn. Thine enemy who spared thee thou didst spare in an ambush, and the friend who walked with thee thou didst sell for a price, and to those who brought thee Love thou didst ever give Lust in thy turn."

And the Man made answer and said, "Even so did I."

And God closed the book of the life of the Man, and said, " Surely I will send thee into Hell. Even into Hell I will send thee."

And the Man cried out, " Thou canst not."

And God said to the Man, " Wherefore can I not send thee to Hell, and for what reason?"

" Because in Hell I have always lived," answered the Man.

And there was silence in the House of Judgment.

And after a space God spake, and said to the Man, " Seeing that I may not send thee into Hell, surely I will send thee unto Heaven.   Even unto Heaven will I send thee."

And the Man cried out, " Thou canst not."

And God said to the Man, " Wherefore can I not send thee unto Heaven, and for what reason?"

" Because never, and in no place, have I been able to imagine it," answered the Man.

And there was silence in the House of Judgment.

Poems in Prose.

XX

EDUCATION

Wilde was at Portora Royal School at Enniskillen until he was
seventeen. In 1871, he went to Trinity College, Dublin, where
he won a Berkeley Gold Medal for Greek, and was elected to a
Queen's Scholarship. In 1874 he went up to Oxford taking a
scholarship at Magdalen. He took a First Class in Classical
Moderations in 1876, and two years later he took a First Class
in Literae Humaniores. He read his Newdigate Prize Poem
" Ravenna " in the Sheldonian Theatre in 1878. These scholastic
accomplishments were sufficient proof of a sound learning but he
was always poor at mathematics.

*

Education is an admirable thing, but it is well to remember
from time to time that nothing that is worth knowing can be
taught.   *The Critic as Artist.*

*

I have forgotten about my schooldays. I have a vague
impression that they were detestable.   *An Ideal Husband.*

*

Ignorance is like a delicate exotic fruit; touch it and the bloom
is gone.   *The Importance of Being Earnest.*

*

In examinations the foolish ask questions that the wise cannot
answer.   *Phrases and Philosophies for the Use of the Young.*

*

The mind of a thoroughly well-informed man is a dreadful
thing. It is like a bric-à-brac shop, all monsters and dust, with
everything priced above its proper value.

The Picture of Dorian Gray.

Give children beauty, not the record of bloody slaughters and barbarous brawls, as they call history, or of the latitude and longitude of places nobody cares to visit, as they call geography.

A Lecture in America.

＊

To have been well brought up is a great drawback nowadays. It shuts one out from so much.   *A Woman of No Importance.*

＊

A school should be the most beautiful place in every town and village—so beautiful that the punishment for undutiful children should be that they should be debarred from going to school the following day.   *In Conversation.*

＊

To know everything about oneself one must know all about others.   *The Critic as Artist.*

＊

. . . in England, at any rate, education produces no effect whatsoever.   If it did, it would prove a serious danger to the upper classes, and would probably lead to acts of violence in Grosvenor Square.   *The Importance of Being Earnest.*

＊

GILBERT : . . . If you meet at dinner a man who has spent his life in educating himself—a rare type in our time, I admit, but still one occasionally to be met with—you rise from the table richer, and conscious that a high ideal has for a moment touched and sanctified your days.   But oh! my dear Ernest, to sit next to a man who has spent his life in trying to educate others!   What a dreadful experience that is!   How appalling is that ignorance which is the inevitable result of imparting opinions!

The Critic as Artist.

＊

LADY BASILDON : Ah! I hate being educated!
MRS. MARCHMONT : So do I.   It puts one almost on a level with the commercial classes.   *An Ideal Husband.*

. . . everybody who is incapable of learning has taken to teaching—that is really what our enthusiasm for education has come to.   *The Decay of Lying.*

*

It is always an advantage not to have received a sound commercial education.   *The Portrait of Mr. W. H.*

*

. . . just as the philanthropist is the nuisance of the ethical sphere, so the nuisance of the intellectual sphere is the man who is so occupied in trying to educate others, that he has never had any time to educate himself.   *The Critic as Artist.*

XXI

ADVICE

Although he once said, " It is always a silly thing to give advice, but to give good advice is absolutely fatal," his advice on everyday affairs was usually very sound.

Before the commencement of his Trials he was advised to go abroad until the trouble had blown over. If he had taken this advice he would probably have avoided the catastrophe that befell him.

*

I always pass on good advice. It is the only thing to do with it. It is never any use to oneself.   *An Ideal Husband.*

*

Don't be conceited about your bad qualities. You may lose them as you grow old.   *A Woman of No Importance.*

*

Find expression for a sorrow, and it will become dear to you. Find expression for a joy, and you intensify its ecstasy.

The Critic as Artist.

*

DUKE : Have prudence; in your dealings with the world. Be not too hasty; act on the second thought, first impulses are generally good.   *The Duchess of Padua.*

*

Never try to pull down public monuments such as the Albert Memorial and the Church. You are sure to be damaged by the falling masonry.   *In Conversation.*

*

Never buy a thing you don't want merely because it is dear.

In Conversation.

It is a dangerous thing to reform anyone.

Lady Windermere's Fan.

*

Wilde's advice, to a youth who had been told that he must begin at the bottom, was—" No, begin at the top and sit upon it."

In Conversation.

*

If you wish for reputation and fame in the world and success during your lifetime, you are right to take every opportunity of advertising yourself. You remember the Latin saying, " Fame springs from one's own house."

In Conversation.

*

Don't be led astray into the paths of virtue.

In Conversation.

*

One should never take sides in anything. Taking sides is the beginning of sincerity and earnestness follows shortly afterwards, and the human being becomes a bore.

A Woman of No Importance.

*

If you wish to understand others you must intensify your own individualism.

The Critic as Artist.

*

About advice:

People are very fond of giving away what they need most themselves. It is what I call the depths of generosity.

The Picture of Dorian Gray.

XXII

SMOKING

He was an inveterate chain-smoker, half-smoking a cigarette and then lighting another.

Robert Sherard records that Wilde used to keep a stock of cigarettes in a large biscuit tin which he carried from room to room.

*

A cigarette is the perfect type of a perfect pleasure. It is exquisite and it leaves one unsatisfied.

The Picture of Dorian Gray.

*

Gold tipped cigarettes are awfully expensive. I can only afford them when I am in debt. *A Woman of No Importance.*

*

Half the pretty women in London smoke cigarettes. Personally I prefer the other half. *An Ideal Husband.*

*

The only use of our attachés is that they supply their friends with excellent tobacco. *The Critic as Artist.*

*

Seeing a " No Smoking " notice in the Academy of Design at Cincinnati, he remarked " Great Heaven! they speak of smoking as if it were a crime. I wonder they don't caution the students not to murder each other on the landings."

In Conversation (America).

LADY BRACKNELL : ... Do you smoke?

JACK : Well, yes, I must admit I smoke.

LADY BRACKNELL : I am glad to hear it. A man should always have an occupation of some kind. There are far too many idle men in London as it is. *The Importance of Being Earnest.*

*

He was once at a dinner party where the ladies had sat too long and he wanted a chance to smoke. His hostess, seeing a lamp which was smouldering, asked him if he would, " Please put it out, Mr. Wilde, it's smoking."

" Happy Lamp." said Wilde. *In Conversation.*

XXIII

FOOD AND DRINK

Wilde was a connoisseur of food and wine, and dined in the best and fashionable places. He delighted in good food and if a meal was well cooked he would send for the chef to congratulate him, another instance of his kindly nature.

He was not addicted to drunkenness, which he regarded as vulgarity. During the last years of his life he suffered violent headaches, and this condition, together with his lowered spirits, induced him to drink to excess. No doubt the drinking of absinthe, to which he had become accustomed, accelerated his death.

*

I have made an important discovery . . . that alcohol, taken in sufficient quantities, produces all the effects of intoxication.

In Conversation.

*

When I am in really great trouble, as anyone who knows me intimately will tell you, I refuse everything except food and drink.

The Importance of Being Earnest.

*

To make a good salad is to be a brilliant diplomatist—the problem is entirely the same in both cases. To know exactly how much oil one must put with one's vinegar.

Vera, or The Nihilists.

*

At dinner, once, a chicken was placed before Oscar. He took up the carvers and after a weary attempt to carve he turned to his wife, and said, " Constance, why do you give me these . . . pedestrians . . . to eat?" *In Conversation.*

Oh, no doubt the cod is a splendid swimmer, admirable for swimming purposes, but not for eating.　　　*In Conversation.*

*

Only dull people are brilliant at breakfast.
　　　　　　　　　　　　　　　　An Ideal Husband.

*

The British cook is a foolish woman—who should be turned for her iniquities into a pillar of salt which she never knows how to use.　　　　　　　　　　*In Conversation.*

*

It is very poor consolation to be told that the man who has given one a bad dinner, or poor wine, is irreproachable in private life.　Even the cardinal virtues cannot atone for half-cold entrées.　　　　　　　*The Picture of Dorian Gray.*

*

An egg is always an adventure : it may be different.
　　　　　　　　　　　　　　　　In Conversation.

*

" Oh, he occasionally takes an alcoholiday."
　　　A remark concerning his brother's fondness for drink.

*

After the first glass of absinthe you see things as you wish they were.　After the second you see them as they are not.　Finally you see things as they really are, and that is the most horrible thing in the world.　I mean disassociated.　Take a top hat.　You think you see it as it really is.　But you don't because you associate it with other things and ideas.　If you had never heard of one before, and suddenly saw it alone, you'd be frightened or you'd laugh.　That is the effect absinthe has, and that is why it drives men mad.　Three nights I sat up all night drinking absinthe, and thinking that I was singularly clear-headed and sane.　The waiter came in and began watering the sawdust.　The most wonderful flowers, tulips, lilies and roses, sprang up, and made a garden in the café " Don't you see them? " I said to him.　" *Mais non, monsieur, il n'y a rien.*"　　　　　　　*In Conversation.*

XXIV

YOUTH AND OLD AGE

Throughout his entire life Wilde was obsessed with the idea of perennial youth and had a continual dread of old age. Sometimes on his birthdays he dressed in deep mourning and jokingly said he was grieving for the passing of another year of his youth. Even in the witness box when facing dire trouble he gave his age as thirty-nine instead of forty-one. Carson pounced on this discrepancy and producing Oscar's birth certificate, pointed out the unreliability of Wilde's evidence.

*

LORD ILLINGWORTH : There is nothing like youth. The middle-aged are mortgaged to Life. The old are in life's lumber room. But youth is the Lord of Life. Youth has a kingdom waiting for it. Everyone is born a king, and most people die in exile, like most kings. To win back my youth . . . there is nothing I wouldn't do—except take exercise, get up early, or be a useful member of the community.   *A Woman of No Importance.*

*

The old believe everything; the middle-aged suspect everything; the young know everything.
      Phrases and Philosophies for the Use of the Young.

*

To get back one's youth, one has merely to repeat one's follies.
      The Picture of Dorian Gray.

*

Youth is the one thing worth having.
      The Picture of Dorian Gray.

The secret of remaining young is never to have an emotion that is unbecoming. *The Picture of Dorian Gray.*

*

The condition of perfection is idleness; the aim of perfection is youth. *Phrases and Philosophies for the Use of the Young.*

*

Youth smiles without any reason. It is one of its chiefest charms. *The Picture of Dorian Gray.*

*

The tragedy of old age is not that one is old, but that one is young. *The Picture of Dorian Gray.*

*

The pulse of joy that beats in us at twenty, becomes sluggish. Our limbs fail, our senses rot. We degenerate into hideous puppets, haunted by the memory of the passions of which we were too much afraid, and the exquisite temptations that we had not the courage to yield to. Youth! Youth! There is absolutely nothing in the world but youth! *The Picture of Dorian Gray.*

*

Youth isn't an affectation. Youth is an art.
An Ideal Husband.

*

It is absurd to talk of the ignorance of youth. The only people to whose opinions I listen now with any respect are people much younger than myself. They seem in front of me.
The Picture of Dorian Gray.

*

The soul is born old but grows young. That is the comedy of life. And the body is born young and grows old. That is life's tragedy. *A Woman of No Importance.*

*

The youth of the present day are quite monstrous. They have absolutely no respect for dyed hair. *Lady Windermere's Fan.*

Wilde once explained the cause of his wearing mourning—
"This happens to be my birthday, and I am mourning, as I shall henceforth do on each of my anniversaries, the flight of one year of my youth into nothingness, the growing blight upon my summer."   *In Conversation.*

XXV

SIN

Wilde was intrigued with the idea of sin as a form of art. The sin for which he suffered was pathological. His greatest sin was indolence.

*

It has been said that the great events of the world take place in the brain. It is in the brain, and the brain only, that the great sins of the world take place. *The Picture of Dorian Gray.*

*

Nothing makes one so vain as being told that one is a sinner.
The Picture of Dorian Gray.

*

Starvation, and not sin, is the parent of modern crime.
The Soul of Man Under Socialism.

*

Sin is a thing that writes itself across a man's face. It cannot be concealed. *The Picture of Dorian Gray.*

*

I can resist everything except temptation.
Lady Windermere's Fan.

*

Wickedness is a myth invented by good people to account for the curious attractiveness of others.
Phrases and Philosophies for the Use of the Young.

*

I hope you have not been leading a double life, pretending to be wicked and being really good all the time, that would be hypocrisy. *The Importance of Being Earnest.*

170

" Lord Henry, I am not at all surprised that the world says that you are extremely wicked."

" But what world says that?" asked Lord Henry, elevating his eyebrows. " It can only be the next world. This world and I are on excellent terms." *The Picture of Dorian Gray.*

*

He hasn't a single redeeming vice. *In Conversation.*

*

The sick do not ask if the hand that smoothes their pillow is pure, nor the dying care if the lips that touch their brow have known the kiss of sin. *A Woman of No Importance.*

*

Every impulse that we strive to strangle broods in the mind and poisons us . . . The only way to get rid of temptation is *to* yield to it. *In Conversation.*

*

. . . there are terrible temptations that it requires strength, strength and courage to yield to. *An Ideal Husband.*

*

If your sins find you out, why worry! It is when they find you *in*, that trouble begins. *In Conversation.*

*

Life's aim, if it has one, is simply to be always looking for temptations. There are not nearly enough. I sometimes pass a whole day without coming across a single one. It is quite dreadful. It makes one so nervous about the future.
                                       A Woman of No Importance.

*

The only difference between the saint and sinner is that every saint has a past, and every sinner has a future.
                                       A Woman of No Importance.

171

Sin is the only real colour-element left in modern life.
The Picture of Dorian Gray.

*

Surely Providence can resist temptation by this time.
Lord Arthur Savile's Crime.

*

Crime in England is rarely the result of sin.   It is nearly always the result of starvation.   *Pen, Pencil and Poison.*

*

There is no sin except stupidity.   *The Critic as Artist.*

*

The body sins once and has done with its sin, for action is a mode of purification.   Nothing remains then but the recollection of a pleasure, or the luxury of a regret.
The Picture of Dorian Gray.

*

One can fancy an intense personality being created out of sin. The fact of a man being a poisoner is nothing against his prose. The domestic virtues are not the true basis of art.
In Conversation.

*

Our criminals are, as a class, so absolutely uninteresting from any psychological point of view.   They are not marvellous Macbeths and terrible Vautrins.   They are merely what ordinary respectable, commonplace people would be if they had not got enough to eat.   *The Soul of Man Under Socialism.*

*

You will soon be going about like the converted, and the revivalist, warning people against all the sins of which you have grown tired.   *The Picture of Dorian Gray.*

As a wicked man I am a complete failure. Why, there are lots
of people who say I have never really done anything wrong in
the whole course of my life. Of course, they only say it behind
my back. *Lady Windermere's Fan.*

*

Nobody ever commits a crime without doing something stupid.
The Picture of Dorian Gray.

*

One should believe evil of everyone, until, of course, people
are found out to be good. But that requires a great deal of
investigation nowadays. *A Woman of No Importance.*

*

FIRST CITIZEN: They will try him first, and sentence him afterwards, will they not, neighbour Anthony?
SECOND CITIZEN: Nay, for he might 'scape his punishment then;
but they will condemn him first so that he gets his deserts, and
give him trial afterwards so that no injustice is done.
The Duchess of Padua.

*

There is only one thing worse than injustice, and that is justice
without her sword in her hand. When right is not might it is
evil. *In Conversation.*

*

XXVI

CRITICISM

Oscar Wilde was the critic as artist in person. He contemplated life and the works of others, and from his impressions created his own motives of art. Criticism as an art is Wilde's unique contribution to Literature.

*

The critic is he who can translate into another manner of a new material his impression of beautiful things. The highest, as the lowest, form of criticism is a mode of autobiography.

The Picture of Dorian Gray.

*

The moment criticism exercises any influence, it ceases to be criticism. The aim of the true critic is to try to chronicle his own moods, not to try to correct the masterpieces of others.

In an Interview.

*

. . . the first duty of an art critic is to hold his tongue at all times, and upon all subjects.   *The English Renaissance of Art.*

*

I am always amused by the silly vanity of those writers and artists of our day who seem to imagine that the primary function of the critic is to chatter about their second-rate work.

The Critic as Artist.

*

The sphere of art and the sphere of ethics are absolutely distinct and separate.   *Reply to a Critic.*

Why should the artist be troubled by the shrill clamour of criticism? Why should those who cannot create take upon themselves to estimate the value of creative work? What can they know about it? If a man's work is easy to understand an explanation is unnecessary.   *The Critic as Artist.*

*

It is exactly because a man cannot do a thing that he is the proper judge of it.   *The Critic as Artist.*

*

Real critics? Ah, how perfectly charming they would be! I am always waiting for their arrival. An inaudible school would be ni e.   *In an Interview.*

*

Criticism demands infinitely more cultivation than creation does.   *The Critic as Artist.*

*

. . . the first step in aesthetic criticism is to realize one's own impressions.   *Pen, Pencil and Poison.*

*

I never reply to my critics. I have far too much time. But I think some day I will give a general answer in the form of a lecture, which I shall call " Straight Talks to Old Men."
          In an Interview.

*

. . . that fine spirit of choice and delicate instinct of selection by which the artist realizes life for us, and gives to it a momentary perfection . . . that spirit of choice, that subtle tact of omission, is really the critical faculty in one of its most characteristic moods, and no one who does not possess this critical faculty can create anything at all in art.   *The Critic as Artist.*

*

When critics disagree the artist is in accord with himself.
          The Picture of Dorian Gray.

175

Yes, there is a terrible moral in *Dorian Gray*—a moral which the prurient will not be able to find in it, but it will be revealed to all whose minds are healthy. Is this an artistic error? I fear it is. It is the only error in the book.   *Reply to a Critic.*

*

My story is an essay on decorative art. It reacts against the crude brutality of plain reason. It is poisonous if you like, but you cannot deny that it is also perfect, and perfection is what we artists aim at.   *Reply to a Critic.*

*

. . . each of the arts has a critic, as it were, assigned to it. The actor is the critic of the drama.   *The Critic as Artist.*

*

The one characteristic of a beautiful form is that one can put into it whatever one wishes, and see in it whatever one chooses to see; and the Beauty, that gives to creation its universal and aesthetic element, makes the critic a creator in his turn, and whispers of a thousand different things which were not present in the mind of him who carved the statue or painted the panel or graved the gem.   *The Critic as Artist.*

*

For a man to be a dramatic critic is as foolish and inartistic as it would be for a man to be a critic of epics or a pastoral critic or a critic of lyrics. All modes of art are one, and the modes of the art that employs words as its medium are quite indivisible. The result of the vulgar specialization of criticism is an elaborate scientific knowledge of the stage—almost as elaborate as that of the stage carpenter and quite on a par with that of the call-boy— combined with an entire incapacity to realize that a play is a work of art or to receive any artistic impressions at all.

In an Interview.

XXVII

SELFISHNESS

Holding out a handful of treasury notes, Wilde once said to Robert Sherard, " You know, I have no sense of property." Indeed a true remark for he was always ready to share what he had with friend, acquaintance and hanger-on.

It is true also that he felt that he was entitled to accept gifts in the same easy way, and during his later years he regarded them as his due. But in his life Oscar Wilde gave away many times more than he received in return.

He was once asked for money by a beggar who said he could not find work and had no bread to eat. Wilde put his hand on the man's shoulder and said, " Now if you had come to me and said that you had work to do, but you couldn't dream of working, and that you had bread to eat, but couldn't think of eating bread, I would have given you two shillings and sixpence— as it is, I give you half a crown! "

*

A red rose is not selfish because it wants to be a red rose. It would be horribly selfish if it wanted all the other flowers in the garden to be both red and roses.

The Soul of Man Under Socialism.

*

There are many things that we would throw away, if we were not afraid that others might pick them up.

The Picture of Dorian Gray.

*

Selfishness is not living as one wishes to live, it is asking others to live as one wishes to live.

The Soul of Man Under Socialism.

*

The most comfortable chair is the one I use myself when I have visitors. *An Ideal Husband.*

XXVIII

RELATIONS

Wilde had a younger sister Isola, who died in childbirth, and an elder brother, William, who died in 1899. It is said that his mother regarded Oscar as being less brilliant than Willie. In fact, overshadowed by Oscar, Willie was resentful of the success of his brother. He once said to George Bernard Shaw, " Oscar was not a man of bad character; you could have trusted him anywhere with a woman."

*

Relations are simply a tedious pack of people, who haven't got the remotest knowledge of how to live, nor the smallest instinct about when to die.   *The Importance of Being Earnest.*

*

I can't help detesting my relations.   I suppose it comes from the fact that none of us can stand other people having the same faults as ourselves.   *The Picture of Dorian Gray.*

*

After a good dinner one can forgive anybody, even one's own relations.   *A Woman of No Importance.*

*

No one cares about distant relations nowadays.   They went out of fashion years ago.   *Lord Arthur Savile's Crime.*

*

Extraordinary thing about the lower classes in England—they are always losing their relations.   They are extremely fortunate in that respect.   *An Ideal Husband.*

XXIX

HEALTH

Wilde enjoyed good health almost all his life and although he disliked being with sick people numerous instances are recorded of his verbal healing powers. Both William Morris and Lord Lytton asked for Oscar Wilde when they were dying. He was the only person apart from their immediate family they could bear to see in their last moments.

*

One knows so well the popular idea of health. The English country-gentleman galloping after a fox—the unspeakable in full pursuit of the uneatable.　　　　*A Woman of No Importance.*

*

Illness of any kind is hardly a thing to be encouraged in others. Health is the primary duty of life.　　*Lady Windermere's Fan.*

*

On being asked if he was ill—" No, not ill, but very weary. The fact is I picked a primrose in the wood yesterday, and it was so ill that I have been sitting up with it all night."

In Conversation.

XXX

PLEASURE

When Wilde was in the witness box he was cross-examined by Edward Carson concerning certain of his axioms from " Phrases and Philosophies for the Use of the Young." One of these phrases was " Pleasure is the only thing one should live for." Carson asked, " Is that true?" Wilde's reply was, " I think that the realization of oneself is the prime aim of life, and to realize oneself through pleasure is finer than to do so through pain. I am, on that point entirely on the side of the ancients—the Greeks. It is a pagan idea." Wilde's answer is a perfect definition of hedonism.

*

Pleasure is the only thing worth having a theory about. But I am afraid I cannot claim my theory as my own. It belongs to Nature, not to me.   *The Picture of Dorian Gray.*

*

An inordinate passion for pleasure is the secret of remaining young.   *Lord Arthur Savile's Crime.*

*

LADY BRACKNELL : . . . I had some crumpets with Lady Harbury, who seems to me to be living entirely for pleasure now.
ALGERNON : I hear her hair has turned quite gold from grief.
                    The Importance of Being Earnest.

*

I adore simple pleasures, they are the last refuge of the complex.   *A Woman of No Importance.*

*

My duty as a gentleman has never interfered with my pleasures in the smallest degree.   *The Importance of Being Earnest.*

180

Knowledge came to me through pleasure, as it always does, I imagine. I was nearly sixteen when the wonder and beauty of the old Greek life began to dawn on me . . . I began to read Greek eagerly for the love of it all, and the more I read the more I was enthralled. *In Conversation.*

*

LORD GORING : I love talking about nothing, father. It is the only thing I know anything about.
LORD CAVERSHAM : You seem to me to be living entirely for pleasure.
LORD GORING : What else is there to live for, father? Nothing ages like happiness. *An Ideal Husband.*

*

" I have never searched for happiness. Who wants happiness? I have searched for pleasure."
" And found it, Mr. Gray? "
" Often. Too often." *The Picture of Dorian Gray.*

*

No civilized man ever regrets a pleasure, and no uncivilized man ever knows what a pleasure is.
The Picture of Dorian Gray.

*

It is better to take pleasure in a rose than to put its root under a microscope. *In Conversation.*

XXXI

WEALTH

*In the Nineties Wilde's earnings reached £8,000 a year—
equal by to-day's standards to an income of at least £50,000. He
indulged himself to excess, he lived extravagantly, bought
expensive presents for friends, never walked even the shortest
distance if a cab was handy; if it was a good one he kept it all
day. Lavish in his hospitality to friends and acquaintances he
spent money with a complete disregard for the future. His belief
that he held a cornucopia in his hands contributed to his undoing.*

*

Young people, nowadays, imagine that money is everything,
and when they grow older they know it.

The Picture of Dorian Gray.

*

Every man of ambition has to fight his century with its own
weapons. What this century worships is wealth. The God of
this century is wealth. To succeed one must have wealth. At
all costs one must have wealth. *An Ideal Husband.*

*

There is always more brass than brains in an aristocracy.

Vera, or The Nihilists.

*

I don't want money. It is only people who pay their bills who
want that, and I never pay mine. *The Picture of Dorian Gray.*

*

LORD ILLINGWORTH : . . . a title is really rather a nuisance in these
democratic days. As George Hartford I had everything I
wanted. Now I have merely everything that other people want,
which isn't nearly so pleasant. *A Woman of No Importance.*

The typical spendthrift is always giving away what he needs most.   *Vera, or The Nihilists.*

*

The English think that a cheque book can solve every problem in life.   *An Ideal Husband.*

*

It is better to have a permanent income than to be fascinating.
                                      The Model Millionaire.

*

When I was at Leadville and reflected that all the shining silver that I saw coming from the mines would be made into ugly dollars, it made me sad.   *In Conversation (America).*

*

Credit is the capital of a younger son.
                                      The Picture of Dorian Gray.

*

One day a tax collector called at Wilde's house in Tite Street.
" Taxes! Why should I pay taxes? " said Wilde.
" But, sir, you are the householder here, are you not? You live here, you sleep here."
" Ah, yes; but then I sleep so badly! "   *In Conversation.*

*

What between the duties expected of one during one's lifetime, and the duties exacted from one after one's death, land has ceased to be either a profit or a pleasure.
                                      The Importance of Being Earnest.

*

Property not merely has duties, but has so many duties that its possession to any large extent is a bore.
                                      The Soul of Man Under Socialism.

Ordinary riches can be stolen from a man.   Real riches cannot.
In the treasury-house of your soul, there are infinitely precious
things that may not be taken from you.

The Soul of Man Under Socialism.

XXXII

POVERTY

He never suffered poverty, although during the greater part of his life he never had sufficient money to suit his extravagant tastes. He had periods of temporary financial embarrassment, as in 1883 when he pawned his Berkeley Gold Medal, but somehow he always managed to extricate himself from his difficulties.

In his earlier life he spoke disparagingly of the poor but as he grew older he became sympathetic towards them. He enjoyed the company of manual workers and they liked him in turn, but it was not until he met them in prison that he appreciated the problems and feelings of the poor.

*

There is only one class in the community that thinks more about money than the rich, and that is the poor. The poor can think of nothing else.   *The Soul of Man Under Socialism.*

*

I should fancy that the real tragedy of the poor is that they can afford nothing but self-denial.   *The Picture of Dorian Gray.*

*

KELVIN: You cannot deny that the House of Commons has always shown great sympathy with the suffering of the poor.
LORD ILLINGWORTH: That is its special vice. That is the special vice of the age. One should sympathize with the joy, the beauty, the colour of life. The less said about life's sores the better.

A Woman of No Importance.

*

Sometimes the poor are praised for being thrifty. But to recommend thrift to the poor is both grotesque and insulting. It is like advising a man who is starving to eat less.

The Soul of Man Under Socialism.

As for the virtuous poor, one can pity them, of course, but one cannot possibly admire them.

The Soul of Man Under Socialism.

*

. . . the East End is a very important problem . . . " It is the problem of slavery, and we try to solve it by amusing the slaves."

The Picture of Dorian Gray.

*

Nowadays we are all of us so hard up, that the only pleasant things to pay *are* compliments. They're the only things we *can* pay.

Lady Windermere's Fan.

*

As for begging it is safer to beg than to take, but it is finer to take than to beg.

The Soul of Man Under Socialism.

*

If the poor only had profiles there would be no difficulty in solving the problem of poverty.

Phrases and Philosophies for the Use of the Young.

*

It is only by not paying one's bills that one can hope to live in the memory of the commercial classes.

Phrases and Philosophies for the Use of the Young.

*

" Are not the rich and poor brothers? " asked the young King. " Ay," answered the man, " and the name of the rich brother is Cain."

The Young King.

*

I am never in during the afternoon, except when I am confined to the house by a sharp attack of penury.

Letter from Paris, May 1898.

XXXIII

FRIENDSHIP

As we grow older we lose that capacity for friendship which we have to such a great degree when we are young. The middle-aged are often made selfish by life's struggle and selfishness is the antithesis of friendship. It is often only when we become old that we realize how we have squandered the alchemic quality of friendship.

Wilde surveyed life through benign, if at times complacent eyes, and he never lost his feeling of benevolence towards the world in general. Friendliness was one of the main characteristics of Wilde's personality and his friends were many and varied. At the time of his trials most of his friends deserted him but a few helped to maintain him after his release from prison. At his bedside when he died were Mr. Robert Ross, Mr. Reginald Turner and the proprietor of the Hotel d'Alsace.

*

Laughter is not at all a bad beginning for a friendship, and it is far the best ending for one.   *The Picture of Dorian Gray.*
*

What is the good of friendship if one cannot say exactly what one means.   *The Devoted Friend.*
*

Between men and women there is no friendship possible. There is passion, enmity, worship, love, but no friendship.
                    Lady Windermere's Fan.
*

An acquaintance that begins with a compliment is sure to develop into a real friendship. It starts in the right manner.
                    An Ideal Husband

One cannot extort affection with a knife. To awaken gratitude in the ungrateful were as vain as to try to waken the dead by cries.
Letter from Paris, June/July 1898.

*

Anybody can sympathize with the sufferings of a friend, but it requires a very fine nature to sympathize with a friend's success. *The Soul of Man Under Socialism.*

*

One has a right to judge a man by the effect he has over his friends. *The Picture of Dorian Gray.*

*

I always like to know everything about my new friends, and nothing about my old ones. *The Picture of Dorian Gray.*

*

I think that generosity is the essence of friendship.
The Devoted Friend.

*

I dare say that if I knew him I should not be his friend at all. It is a very dangerous thing to know one's friends.
The Remarkable Rocket.

*

I would sooner lose my best friend than my worst enemy. To have friends, you know, one need only be good-natured; but when a man has no enemy left there must be something mean about him. *Vera, or The Nihilists.*

*

I choose my friends for their good looks, my acquaintances for their good characters, and my enemies for their good intellects. I have not got one who is a fool. They are all men of some intellectual power, and consequently they all appreciate me.
The Picture of Dorian Gray.

She is without one good quality, she lacks the finest spark of decency, and is quite the wickedest woman in London. I haven't a word to say in her favour . . . and she is one of my greatest friends. *In Conversation.*

*

Robert gave Harry a terrible black eye, or Harry gave him one; I forget which, but I know they were great friends.

In Conversation.

*

The absence of old friends one can endure with equanimity. But even a momentary separation from anyone to whom one has just been introduced is almost unbearable.

The Importance of Being Earnest.

*

I shall never make a new friend in my life, though perhaps a few after I die. *In Conversation.*

XXXIV

MORALS

Morals played a small part in the life of Oscar Wilde, and George Bernard Shaw once said to Lord Alfred Douglas, " If ever there was a writer whose prayer to posterity might well have been ' Read my works and let my life alone,' it was Oscar." Wilde himself, in his essay on Wainwright, says, " The fact of a man being a poisoner is nothing against his prose." He was amoral and regarded manners as being of more importance than morals.

*

If you pretend to be good, the world takes you very seriously. If you pretend to be bad, it doesn't. Such is the astounding stupidity of optimism.   *Lady Windermere's Fan.*

*

Morality is simply the attitude we adopt to people whom we personally dislike.   *An Ideal Husband.*

*

When we are happy we are always good, but when we are good we are not always happy.   *The Picture of Dorian Gray.*

*

It is personalities, not principles, that move the age.

In Conversation.

*

. . . intellectual generalities are always interesting, but generalities in morals mean absolutely nothing.

A Woman of No Importance.

190

Good resolutions are useless attempts to interfere with scientific laws. Their origin is pure vanity. Their result is absolutely nil. They give us, now and then, some of those luxurious sterile emotions that have a certain charm for the weak. That is all that can be said of them. They are simply cheques that men draw on a bank where they have no account.

The Picture of Dorian Gray.

*

I never came across anyone in whom the moral sense was dominant who was not heartless, cruel, vindictive, log-stupid, and entirely lacking in the smallest sense of humanity. Moral people, as they are termed, are simple beasts. I would sooner have fifty unnatural vices than one unnatural virtue.

In Conversation.

*

To be good, according to the vulgar standard of goodness, is obviously quite easy. It merely requires a certain amount of sordid terror, a certain lack of imaginative thought, and a certain low passion for middle-class respectability.

The Critic as Artist.

*

It is not good for one's morals to see bad acting.

The Picture of Dorian Gray.

*

Modern morality consists in accepting the standard of one's age. I consider that for any man of culture to accept the standard of his age is a form of the grossest immorality.

The Picture of Dorian Gray.

*

Several plays have been written lately that deal with the monstrous injustice of the social code of morality at the present time. It is indeed a burning shame that there should be one law for men and another law for women. I think there should be no law for anybody.

In an Interview.

Self-sacrifice is a thing that should be put down by law. It is so demoralizing to the people for whom one sacrifices oneself. They always go to the bad. *An Ideal Husband.*

*

You can't make people good by Act of Parliament—that is something. *In Conversation.*

*

Nothing is more painful to me than to come across virtue in a person in whom I have never expected its existence. It is like finding a needle in a bundle of hay. It pricks you. If we have a virtue we should warn people of it. *In Conversation.*

*

We think that we are generous because we credit our neighbours with the possession of those virtues that are likely to be a benefit to us. *In Conversation.*

*

" I am rather afraid that I have annoyed him," answered the Linnet. " The fact is that I have told him a story with a moral." "Ah! that is always a very dangerous thing to do," said the Duck. And I quite agree with her. *The Devoted Friend.*

XXXV

TRUTH

Wilde was always ready to sacrifice truth for the sake of an epigram and to draw upon his imagination to make his point in a story, although he describes as " loathsome " the memory of the lies he told to his solicitor, Humphreys, before his trials, when in the ghastly glare of a bleak room he sat with a serious face telling serious lies to a bald man.

*

To know the truth one must imagine myriads of falsehoods. For what is Truth? *The Critic as Artist.*

*

If one tells the truth, one is sure, sooner or later, to be found out. *Phrases and Philosophies for the Use of the Young.*

*

It is a terrible thing for a man to find out suddenly that all his life he has been speaking nothing but the truth.

The Importance of Being Earnest.

*

I could never have dealings with Truth. If Truth were to come unto me, to my room, he would say to me " You are too wilful." And I would say to him, " You are too obvious." And I should throw him out of the window!

You would say to him, " Is not Truth a woman? "

Then I could not throw her out of the window; I should bow her to the door. *In Conversation.*

*

The truth is rarely pure and never simple. Modern life would be very tedious if it were either, and modern literature a complete impossibility. *The Importance of Being Earnest.*

Many a young man starts in life with a natural gift for exaggeration which, if nurtured in congenial and sympathetic surroundings, or by the imitation of the best models, might grow into something really great and wonderful. But, as a rule, he comes to nothing. He either falls into careless habits of accuracy, or takes to frequenting the society of the aged and well-informed. Both things are equally fatal to his imagination, as indeed they would be to the imagination of anybody, and in a short time he develops a morbid and unhealthy faculty of truth-telling, begins to verify all statements made in his presence, has no hesitation in contradicting people who are much younger than himself, and often ends by writing novels which are so life-like that no one can possibly believe in their probability.　　*The Decay of Lying.*

*

People have a careless way of talking about a " born liar," just as they talk about a born poet. Lying and poetry are arts— arts as Plato saw, not unconnected with each other—and they require the most careful study, the most interested devotion.
The Decay of Lying.

*

. . . a thing is not necessarily true because a man dies for it.
The Portrait of Mr. W. H.

*

Man is least himself when he talks in his own person. Give him a mask, and he will tell you the truth.
The Critic as Artist.

*

The telling of beautiful untrue things, is the proper aim of Art.
The Decay of Lying.

*

A truth ceases to be true when more than one person believes in it.　　*Phrases and Philosophies for the Use of the Young.*

As for believing things, I can believe anything, provided that it is quite incredible.   *The Picture of Dorian Gray.*

*

He would be the best of fellows if he did not always speak the truth.   *The Sphinx without a Secret.*

*

It is enough that our fathers have believed. They have exhausted the faith-faculty of the species. Their legacy to us is the scepticism of which they were afraid.   *In Conversation.*

*

On " Patience " to a New York Audience:
You have listened to the charming music of Mr. Sullivan and the clever satire of Mr. Gilbert for three hundred nights, and I am sure it is not too much to ask you, after having given so much time to satire, to listen to the truth for one evening.
                    Lecturing in America.

*

In modern life nothing produces such an effect as a good platitude. It makes the whole world kin.   *An Ideal Husband.*

*

. . . the truth is a thing I get rid of as soon as possible! Bad habit, by the way. Makes one very unpopular at the club . . with the older members. They call it being conceited.
                    An Ideal Husband.

*

The things one feels absolutely certain about are never true. That is the fatality of Faith, and the lesson of Romance.
                    The Picture of Dorian Gray.

*

After all, what is a fine lie! Simply that which is its own evidence.   *The Decay of Lying.*

195

Vulgarity is simply the conduct of other people and falsehoods the truths of other people. *An Ideal Husband.*

*

... I am prevented from coming in consequence of a subsequent engagement. I think that would be a rather nice excuse; it would have all the surprise of candour. *The Picture of Dorian Gray.*

XXXVI

HISTORY

He delighted in History, both the factual sort and his own imaginative versions of past events. In his conversation the two kinds were indistinguishable, and he loved to trace a story through history embellishing and inventing on the way.

*

The one duty we owe to history is to rewrite it.
The Critic as Artist.

*

To give an accurate description of what has never occurred is not merely the proper occupation of the historian, but the inalienable privilege of any man of parts and culture.
The Critic as Artist.

*

As one reads history . . . one is absolutely sickened, not by the crimes that the wicked have committed, but by the punishments that the good have inflicted; and a community is infinitely more brutalized by the habitual employment of punishment than it is by the occasional occurrence of crime.   *In Conversation.*

*

The only form of fiction in which real characters do not seem out of place is history.   In novels they are detestable.
In Conversation.

*

Anybody can make history.   Only a great man can write it.
The Critic as Artist.

You give the criminal calendar of Europe to your children under the name of history. *A Lecture in America.*

*

The ages live in history through their anachronisms.
Phrases and Philosophies for the Use of the Young.

*

My *forte* is more in writing pamphlets than in taking shots. Still a regicide has always a place in history.
Vera, or The Nihilists.

XXXVII

SOCIETY

Wilde loved " high society " and certainly at the pinnacle of his success the socialites delighted in his talk. Later, he despised " high society", loathed the middle classes and it was only to the poor that he showed sympathy.

✳

Never speak disrespectfully of society. Only people who can't get into it do that. *In Conversation.*

✳

LORD CAVERSHAM: Can't make out how you stand London Society. The thing has gone to the dogs, a lot of damned nobodies talking about nothing. *An Ideal Husband.*

✳

Society, civilized society at least, is never very ready to believe anything to the detriment of those who are both rich and fascinating. *The Picture of Dorian Gray.*

✳

If one could only teach the English how to talk, and the Irish how to listen, society here would be quite civilised.
An Ideal Husband.

✳

" To get into the best society nowadays one has either to feed people, amuse people, or shock people—that is all."
In Conversation.

✳

Society often forgives the criminal; it never forgives the dreamer. *The Critic as Artist.*

Everybody one meets is a paradox nowadays. It is a great bore. It makes society so obvious. *An Ideal Husband.*

*

What is interesting about people in good society is the mask that each one of them wears, not the reality that lies behind the mask. *The Decay of Lying.*

*

Our Society is terribly over-populated. Really, someone should arrange a proper scheme of assisted emigration.

An Ideal Husband.

*

I love London Society! I think it has immensely improved. It is entirely composed now of beautiful idiots and brilliant lunatics. Just what Society should be. *An Ideal Husband.*

*

Each class preaches the importance of those virtues it need not exercise. The rich harp on the value of thrift, the idle grow eloquent over the dignity of labour. *In Conversation.*

*

A child can understand a punishment inflicted by an individual, such as a parent or guardian, and bear it with a certain amount of acquiesence. What it cannot understand is a punishment inflicted by society. *Letter to the Daily Chronicle.*

XXXVIII

GENIUS

Oscar never doubted his own genius. He was conscious always of his own powers and his own intellectual superiority over his contemporaries. He craved recognition of this, to him obvious, quality of genius and expended energies in his conversation in convincing others of his distinction; energies that would have been better employed in creating in literature a more adequate record of his powers than his works indicate.

The tragedy of Wilde is not that he suffered personally, and fell from the heights to the depths; that was his loss. The tragedy is that he dissipated the genius that was within him; that was the World's loss.

" The Importance of Being Earnest ", his last and best play, written in less than a month at Worthing, is an indication of the real capabilities of Wilde as a playwright. This play apart from other works, is an indication of that individually light-hearted quality of genius that Wilde undoubtedly possessed. " Earnest " is a refutation in itself of any suggestion that Wilde was ' written-out ' and is a foretaste of what would surely have been written had not inexcusable self-indulgence, weak moral fibre and mental sickness precipitated his end.

*

Geniuses . . . are always talking about themselves, when I want them to be thinking about me.   *An Ideal Husband.*

*

The public is wonderfully tolerant.   It forgives everything except genius.   *The Critic as Artist.*

*

I like looking at geniuses, and listening to beautiful people.
      An Ideal Husband.

201

Would you like to know the great drama of my life? It is that I have put my genius into my life—I have put only my talent into my works. *In Conversation.*

*

Genius is born, not paid. *In Conversation.*

*

I know so many men in London whose only talent is for washing. I suppose that is why men of genius so seldom wash, they are afraid of being mistaken for men of talent only! *In Conversation.*

*

Not being a genius, he had no enemies.
Lord Arthur Savile's Crime.

*

Indifference is the revenge the world takes on mediocrities.
Vera, or The Nihilists.

*

Caricature is the tribute mediocrity pays to genius.
A Lecture in America.

*

For a man to be both a genius and a Scotsman is the very stage for tragedy . . . Your Scotsman believes only in success . . . God saved the genius of Robert Burns to poetry by driving him through drink to failure. *In Conversation.*

*

Don't talk to me about the hardships of the poor. The hardships of the poor are necessities; but talk to me about the hardships of the men of genius, and I could weep tears of blood.
In Conversation.

*

Were men as intelligent as bees, all gifted individuals would be supported by the community, as the bees support the Queen. We should be the first charge on the state. Just as Socrates declared that he should be kept in the Prytaneum at the public's expense.
In Conversation.

LORD GORING : . . . I am delighted at what you tell me about
Robert . . . It shows he has got pluck.
LORD CAVERSHAM : He has got more than pluck, sir, he has got
genius.
LORD GORING : Ah ! I prefer pluck. It is not so common,
nowadays. *An Ideal Husband.*

*

The worst thing you can do for a person of genius is to help
him : that way lies his destruction. I have had many devoted
helpers—and you see the result. *In Conversation.*

*

Every great man nowadays has his disciples and it is always
Judas who writes the biography. *The Critic as Artist.*

*

FRANK (HARRIS) insists on my being always at high intellectual
pressure—it is most exhausting—but when we arrive at Napoule
I am going to break the news to him—now an open secret—that I
have softening of the brain—and cannot always be a genius.
Letter from Paris, December 1898.

XXXIX

BEAUTY

To Wilde, Beauty was a Religion. He was once introduced to a woman who took pride in her ugliness. She asked him, "Tell me, don't men think I am the ugliest woman in Paris?" Wilde bowed courteously and replied, "No, madam, in all the world."

He said later that for once he was able to please a woman by telling her the truth.

*

Beauty is a form of Genius—is higher, indeed, than Genius as it needs no explanation.   *The Picture of Dorian Gray.*

*

Beauty, real beauty, ends where an intellectual expression begins. Intellect is in itself a mode of exaggeration and destroys the harmony of any face. The moment one sits down to think, one becomes all nose, or all forehead, or something horrid. Look at the successful men in any of the learned professions. How perfectly hideous they are! Except, of course in the Church. But then in the Church they don't think. A bishop keeps on saying at the age of eighty what he was told to say when he was eighteen, and as a natural consequence he always looks delightful.
       The Picture of Dorian Gray.

*

To be perfectly proportioned is a rare thing in an age when so many women are either over life-size or insignificant.
       Lord Arthur Savile's Crime.

*

I think that it is better to be beautiful than to be good. But on the other hand no one is more ready than I am to acknowledge that it is better to be good than to be ugly.
       The Picture of Dorian Gray.

To be pretty is the best fashion there is, and the only fashion that England succeeds in setting. *An Ideal Husband.*

*

Have I not stood face to face with beauty, that is enough for one man's life. *The Duchess of Padua.*

*

Good looks are a snare that every sensible man would like to be caught in. *The Importance of Being Earnest.*

*

To discern the beauty of a thing is the finest point to which we can arrive. Even a colour-sense is more important, in the development of the individual, than a sense of right and wrong. *The Critic as Artist.*

*

All beautiful things belong to the same age.
Pen, Pencil and Poison.

*

To look at anything that is inconstant is charming nowadays.
A Woman of No Importance.

*

At twilight nature becomes a wonderfully suggestive effect, and is not without loveliness, though perhaps its chief use is to illustrate quotations from the poets. *The Decay of Lying.*

*

Beauty has as many meanings as man has moods. Beauty is the symbol of symbols. Beauty reveals everything, because it expresses nothing. When it shows us itself it shows us the whole fiery-coloured world. *The Critic as Artist.*

*

Even men of the noblest possible moral character are extremely susceptible to the influence of the physical charms of others.
The Importance of Being Earnest.

She has the remains of really remarkable ugliness.

In Conversation.

*

When I look at the map and see what an ugly country Australia is, I feel that I want to go there and see if it cannot be changed into a more beautiful form!   *In Conversation.*

*

Those who find ugly meanings in beautiful things are corrupt without being charming.   That is a fault.

Those who find beautiful meanings in beautiful things are the cultivated.   For these there is hope.

They are the elect to whom beautiful things mean only Beauty.

The Picture of Dorian Gray.

XL

THOUGHT

Wilde considered thought to be more important than action, and regarded contemplation as the most cultured way of living. When at home, he spent hours, lying on a sofa, expending his energies in thought.

*

All thought is immoral. Its very essence is destruction. If you think of anything, you kill it. Nothing survives being thought of.   *A Woman of No Importance.*

*

The value of an idea has nothing whatsoever to do with the sincerity of the man who expresses it.
     The Picture of Dorian Gray.

*

Yes: I am a dreamer. For a dreamer is one who can only find his way by moonlight, and his punishment is that he sees the dawn before the rest of the world.   *The Critic as Artist.*

*

The boy-burglar is simply the inevitable result of life's imitative instinct. He is Fact, occupied as Fact usually is, with trying to reproduce Fiction, and what we see in him is repeated on an extended scale throughout the whole of life. Schopenhauer has analysed the pessimism that characterizes modern thought, but Hamlet invented it. The world has become sad because a puppet was once melancholy.   *The Decay of Lying.*

*

Consistency is the last refuge of the unimaginative.
     In Conversation.

It is only the dull who like practical jokes. *In Conversation.*

*

Whenever I think of my bad qualities at night, I go to sleep at once. *In Conversation.*

*

Wisdom comes with winters. *A Florentine Tragedy.*

*

The reason we all like to think so well of others is that we are all afraid for ourselves. The basis of optimism is sheer terror. We think that we are generous because we credit our neighbour with the possession of those virtues that are likely to be a benefit to us. We praise the banker that we may overdraw our account, and find good qualities in the highwayman in the hope that he may spare our pockets. *The Picture of Dorian Gray.*

*

. . . To the true cynic nothing is ever revealed.

In Conversation.

*

While, in the opinion of society, contemplation is the gravest thing of which any citizen can be guilty, in the opinion of the highest culture it is the proper occupation of man.

The Critic as Artist.

*

An idea that is not dangerous is unworthy of being called an idea at all. *The Critic as Artist.*

*

Nothing refines but the intellect.

A Woman of No Importance.

*

Conscience must be merged in instinct before we become fine.

In Conversation.

Only the shallow know themselves.
Phrases and Philosophies for the Use of the Young.

*

A man who does not think for himself does not thing at all. It is grossly selfish to require of one's neighbour that he should think in the same way. *The Soul of Man Uuder Socialism.*

*

Thinking is the most unhealthy thing in the world, and people die of it just as they die of any other disease. Fortunately, in England at any rate, thought is not catching. Our splendid physique as a people is entirely due to our national stupidity.
The Decay of Lying.

*

Savages seem to have quite the same views as cultured people on almost all subjects. They are excessively advanced.
A Woman of No Importance.

*

Men of thought should have nothing to do with action.
Vera, or The Nihilists.

*

It is only about things that do not interest one that one can find a really unbiased opinion, which is no doubt the reason why an unbiased opinion is always absolutely valueless.
The Critic as Artist.

*

"What are you thinking?" is the only question that any civilized being should ever be allowed to whisper to another.
The Critic as Artist.

*

What seems to us bitter trials are often blessings in disguise.
The Importance of Being Earnest.

The only thing which sustains one through life is the consciousness of the immense inferiority of everybody else, and this feeling I have always cultivated.   *The Remarkable Rocket.*

*

I can stand brute force, but brute reason is quite unreasonable. There is something unfair about its use.   It is hitting below the intellect.   *The Picture of Dorian Gray.*
*

Of what use is it to a man to travel sixty miles an hour?   Is he any the better for it?   Why, a fool can buy a railway ticket and travel sixty miles an hour.   Is he any the less a fool!
                                                    A Lecture in America.
*

Seriousness is the only refuge of the shallow!
                                                    In Conversation.
*

Those who see any difference between soul and body have neither.   *Phrases and Philosophies for the Use of the Young.*

*

The dreams of the great middle classes of this country, as recorded in Mr. Myer's two bulky volumes on the subject, and the Transactions of the Psychical Society, are the most depressing things I have ever read.   There is not even a fine nightmare among them.   They are commonplace, sordid and tedious.
                                                    The Decay of Lying.
*

Action!   What is action?   It dies at the moment of its energy. It is a base concession to fact.   The world is made by the singer for the dreamer!   *In Conversation.*
*

Action is limited and relative.   Unlimited and absolute is the vision of him who sits at ease and watches, who walks in loneliness and dreams.   *In Conversation.*

Nothing can cure the soul but the senses, just as nothing can cure the senses but the soul. *The Picture of Dorian Grey.*

*

Intellect is in itself a mode of exaggeration, and destroys the harmony of any face. The moment one sits down to think, one becomes all nose, or all forehead, or something horrid.

The Picture of Dorian Gray.

XLI

SYMPATHY

His sympathy with the troubles of others is proverbial, and he did not confine his sympathies to verbal condolences. Instead he was always eager to render help by deed or by monetary assistance.

*

All sympathy is fine, but sympathy with suffering is the least fine mode. There is in it a certain element of terror for our own safety.   *In Conversation.*

*

If there was less sympathy in the world there would be less trouble in the world.   *An Ideal Husband.*

*

There is always something infinitely mean about other people's tragedies.   *The Picture of Dorian Gray.*

*

I am always thinking about myself, and I expect everybody else to do the same. That is what is called sympathy.
                                                The Remarkable Rocket.

*

It must be remembered that while sympathy with joy intensifies the sum of joy in the world, sympathy with pain does not really diminish the amount of pain. It may make man better able to endure evil, but the evil remains.
                              The Soul of Man Under Socialism.

I consider ugliness a kind of malady, and illness and suffering always inspire me with revulsion. A man with the toothache ought, I know, to have my sympathy, for it is a terrible pain, yet he fills me with nothing but aversion. He is tedious; he is a bore; I cannot stand him; I cannot look at him; I must get away from him. *In Conversation.*

*

I can sympathize with everything, except suffering. I cannot sympathize with that. It is too ugly, too horrible, too distressing. There is something terribly morbid in the modern sympathy with pain. One should sympathize with the colour, the beauty; the joy of life. The less said about life's sores the better.
The Picture of Dorian Gray.

*

I have learned now that pity is the greatest and the most beautiful thing in the world, and that is why I cannot bear ill-will towards those who caused my suffering and those who condemned me; no, nor to anyone, because without them I should not have known all that. *In Conversation at Berneval.*

XLII

GAMES

He neither enjoyed playing games nor was he interested in watching them being played. Riding was the only exercise he took and this only in his younger days. Despite his lack of interest in sporting activities he was surprisingly strong. On one occasion at Magdalen a party of boisterous fellow-students decided to rag Wilde and smash up his room. He gave them a much hotter reception than they had expected and unceremoniously tossed the first four young gentlemen, one after another, into the corridor. That was the end of the ragging of Wilde. Afterwards he invited the chastened young men into his study for a drink and soon they were thoroughly enjoying his company.

*

I am afraid I play no outdoor games at all, except dominoes . . .
I have sometimes played dominoes outside French cafés.

In Conversation.

*

On being asked if he ever went in for games at school.
No, I never liked to kick or be kicked.   *In Conversation.*

*

Football is all very well as a game for rough girls, but it is hardly suitable for delicate boys.   *In Conversation.*

*

The only possible form of exercise is to talk, not to walk . . .

In an Interview.

XLIII

EMOTIONS

Wilde was acutely emotional and his feelings readily brimmed to the surface whether in laughter or in tears. His emotions, however, were not necessarily selfishly stirred, nor the result of his inherent exhibitionism, for he sympathized with the misfortunes of others and felt their sufferings acutely.

This sensibility is not represented in his plays, for in these he was more concerned with brilliant superficialities than with harrowing reality and his characters lack any real depth of feeling. They are stylish puppets dancing to the music of his words.

It must be noticed however that even in his apparently most trivial remarks there is usually a sting of truth which gives an indication of his understanding of human nature, for ' home truths ' are the result of insight into the frailties of character.

Occasionally he was pettish and revealed all the foibles of nature found in a person to whom fame has come too easily. Success went to his head and often he adopted an air of annoying arrogance which was out of keeping with his real nature, for beneath the surface there existed a deeper emotional understanding than his plays or his bizarre façade indicated. This appreciation of human feelings is exemplified in his two letters to the " Daily Chronicle ", ' The Soul of Man Under Socialism ', ' The Ballad of Reading Gaol ', and certain portions of ' De Profundis '. It was probably this acute sensitivity coupled with an insatiable desire for new sensations that upset his mental and moral balance.

*

. . . emotion for the sake of emotion is the aim of art, and emotion for the sake of action is the aim of life.

The Critic as Artist.

215

It is only shallow people who require years to get rid of an emotion. A man who is master of himself, can end a sorrow as easily as he can invent a pleasure. *The Picture of Dorian Gray.*

*

A woman's life revolves in curves of emotion. It is upon lines of intellect that a man's life progresses. *An Ideal Husband.*

*

. . . a sentimentalist is simply one who desires to have the luxury of an emotion without paying for it. *In Conversation.*

*

The advantage of the emotions is that they lead us astray, and the advantage of science is that it is not emotional.
The Picture of Dorian Gray.

*

I cannot repeat an emotion. No one can, except senti-
mentalists. *The Picture of Dorian Gray.*

*

One could never pay too high a price for any sensation.
The Picture of Dorian Gray.

*

Moods don't last. It is their chief charm.
A Woman of No Importance.

*

The tears that we shed at a play are a type of the exquisite sterile emotions that it is the function of Art to awaken. We weep but we are not wounded. We grieve but our grief is not bitter.
The Critic as Artist.

XLIV

TIME

Wilde was reliably unpunctual. He once arrived late at a luncheon party and to his hostess, who reproved him, he said—" and how, Madam, can that little clock know what the great golden sun is doing? "

*

When one pays a visit it is for the purpose of wasting other people's time, not one's own.   *An Ideal Husband.*

*

Time is waste of money.
            Phrases and Philosophies for the Use of the Young.

*

Punctuality is the thief of·time—I am not punctual myself, but I do like punctuality in others.   *In Conversation.*

*

I would sooner lose a train by the ABC than catch it by Bradshaw.   *In Conversation.*

*

I am due at the club.   It is the hour when we sleep there.
                        In Conversation.

*

Everybody seems in a hurry to catch a train.   This is a state of things which is not favourable to poetry or romance.
                        In Conversation (America).

XLV

WORK

Wilde only worked because he needed money to spend his time doing nothing, but talk. He claimed that the six weeks he spent writing " Dorian Gray " was the longest time he spent on any of his works. He believed that work was the refuge of people who had nothing better to do.

*

Work is the curse of the drinking classes.   *In Conversation.*

*

It is always with the best intentions that the worst work is done.
                                          The Critic as Artist.

*

It is mentally and morally injurious to a man to do anything in which he does not find pleasure, and many forms of labour are quite pleasureless activities and should be regarded as such . . . Man is made for something better than disturbing dirt. All work of that kind should be done by a machine.
                        The Soul of Man Under Socialism.

*

It is very vulgar to talk about one's business. Only people like stockbrokers do that, and then merely at dinner-parties.
                        The Importance of Being Earnest.

*

I was working on the proof of one of my poems all the morning, and took out a comma. In the afternoon I put it back again.
                                          In Conversation.

We live in the age of the overworked, and the under-educated; the age in which people are so industrious that they become absolutely stupid.   *The Critic as Artist.*

*

Industry is the root of all ugliness.
                    Phrases and Philosophies for the Use of the Young.

*

A cook and a diplomatist! an excellent parallel. If I had a son who was a fool I'd make him one or the other.
                    Vera, or The Nihilists.

*

Printing is so dull. There is nothing exquisite about it at present. In my next publication I am hoping to give examples of something more satisfying in this way. The letters shall be of a rare design; the commas will be sunflowers, and the semicolons pomegranates.   *In Conversation.*

*

Cultivated leisure is the aim of man.
                    The Soul of Man Under Socialism.

*

It is to do nothing that the elect exist.   *The Critic as Artist.*

*

Nobody else's work gives me any suggestion. It is only by entire isolation from everything that one can do any work. Idleness gives one the mood in which to write, isolation the conditions. Concentration on oneself recalls the new and wonderful world that one presents in the colour and cadence of words in movement.   *In an Interview.*

*

Up to the present, man has been, to a certain extent, the slave of machinery, and there is something tragic in the fact that as soon as a man had invented a machine to do his work he began to starve.   *The Soul of Man Under Socialism.*

He rides in the Row at ten o'clock in the morning, goes to the Opera three times a week, changes his clothes at least five times a day, and dines out every night of the season.   You don't call that leading an idle life, do you?   *An Ideal Husband.*

*

There is something tragic about the enormous number of young men there are in England at the present moment who start life with perfect profiles, and end by adopting some useful profession.
                    Phrases and Philosophies for the Use of the Young.

*

Action, indeed, is always easy, and when presented to us in its most aggravated, because most continuous, form, which I take to be that of real industry, becomes simply the refuge of people who have nothing whatever to do.   *The Critic as Artist.*

XLVI

EXPERIENCE

Wilde shows us the figure of a man hurrying through life feverishly tasting experiences with an insatiable appetite. He said, whilst at Oxford, " I want to eat of the fruit of all the trees in the garden of the world." In a short life he almost succeeded, but instead of gaining, Wilde lost by his experiences.

*

Experience is the name every one gives to their mistakes.
Lady Windermere's Fan.

*

Personal experience is a most vicious and limited circle.
The Decay of Lying.

*

We always misunderstood ourselves and rarely understood others. Experience was of no ethical value. It was merely the name men gave to their mistakes. *The Picture of Dorian Gray.*

*

Experience is a question of instinct about life.
In Conversation.

221

XLVII

THE TRIALS

Oscar Wilde's three trials are a notable cause célèbre *and take an important place in legal history. The First Trial opened on Wednesday, 3rd April, 1895; the Second Trial on Friday, 26th April, 1895; and the Third Trial on Monday, 20th May, 1895. Five days later Wilde was found guilty on all counts except one, and was sentenced to two years' hard labour.*

Oscar Wilde's duel of wits with Edward Carson, the greatest cross-examiner of his day showed the brilliance of Wilde's epigrammatic repartée. He more than held his own on literary ground but when face-to-face with the irrefutable truth of the allegations against him he was stunned, and collapsed under the remorseless questioning of Carson.

Whilst in prison Wilde wrote that all trials are trials for one's life, just as all sentences are sentences of death.

*

Wilde was advised to go abroad to avoid the trial—his reply. "Everyone wants me to go abroad. I have just been abroad, and now I have come home again. One can't keep going abroad, unless one is a missionary, or, what comes to the same thing, a commercial traveller." *In Conversation.*

*

When Wilde was told that he would be cross-examined by Edward Carson (who had been a fellow-student at Trinity College, Dublin) he replied: "No doubt he will perform his task with all the added bitterness of an old friend."

In Conversation.

*

He tells me that he (Willie his brother) is defending me all over London. My poor dear brother could compromise a steam-engine. *In Conversation.*

222

THE FIRST TRIAL

Wilde was questioned by Sir Edward Clarke concerning a blackmailer who had called at Wilde's house about a letter which Wilde had written to Lord Alfred Douglas.

*

Sir Edward Clarke :

What happened at that interview?

Oscar Wilde :

I felt that this was the man who wanted money from me. I said, " I suppose you have come about my beautiful letter to Lord Alfred Douglas. If you had not been so foolish as to send a copy of it to Mr. Beerbohm Tree, I would glady have paid you a very large sum of money for the letter, as I consider it to be a work of art." He said, " A very curious construction can be put on that letter." I said in reply, " Art is rarely intelligible to the criminal classes." He said, " A man offered me £60 for it." I said to him, " If you take my advice you will go to that man and sell my letter to him for £60. I myself have never received so large a sum for any prose work of that length; but I am glad to find that there is someone in England who considers a letter of mine worth £60." He was somewhat taken aback by my manner, perhaps, and said, " The man is out of town." I replied, " He is sure to come back," and I advised him to get the £60. He then changed his manner a little, saying that he had not a single penny and that he had been on many occasions trying to find me. I said that I could not guarantee his cab expenses, but that I would gladly give him half a sovereign. He took the money and went away.

Sir Edward Clarke :

Was anything said about a sonnet?

Oscar Wilde :

Yes. I said, " The letter, which is a prose poem, will shortly be published in sonnet form in a delightful magazine, and I will send you a copy of it."

SIR EDWARD CLARKE:

As a matter of fact, the letter was the basis of a French poem that was published in *The Spirit Lamp*?

OSCAR WILDE:

Yes.

SIR EDWARD CLARKE:

It is signed " Pierre Louÿs." Is that the *nom de plume* of a friend of yours?

OSCAR WILDE:

Yes, a young French poet of great distinction, a friend of mine, who has lived in England.

SIR EDWARD CLARKE:

Did Allen then go away?

OSCAR WILDE:

Yes, and in about five minutes Cliburn came to the house. I went out to him and said, " I cannot bother any more about this matter." He produced the letter out of his pocket saying, " Allen has asked me to give it back to you." I did not take it immediately, but asked: " Why does Allen give me back this letter?" He said, " Well, he says that you were kind to him, and there is no use trying to ' rent '* you as you only laugh at us." I took the letter and said, " I will accept it back, and you can thank Allen from me for all the anxiety he has shown about it." I looked at the letter, and saw that it was extremely soiled. I said to him, " I think it is quite unpardonable that better care was not taken of this original manuscript of mine." He said he was very sorry, but it had been in many hands. I gave him half a sovereign for his trouble, and then said, " I am afraid you are leading a wonderfully wicked life." He said, " There is good and bad in everyone of us." I told him he was a born philosopher, and he then left.

*　　　*　　　*

Later in the examination Wilde was asked what took place when Lord Queensberry visited his house, accompanied by another man (who was a pugilist).

* Blackmail.

OSCAR WILDE :

At the end of June, 1894, there was an interview between myself and Lord Queensberry in my house. He called upon me, not by appointment, about four o'clock in the afternoon, accompanied by a gentleman with whom I was not acquainted. The interview took place in my library. Lord Queensberry was standing by the window. I walked over to the fireplace, and he said to me, " Sit down." I said to him, " I do not allow anyone to talk like that to me in my house or anywhere else. I suppose you have come to apologize for the statement you made about my wife and myself in letters you wrote to your son. I should have the right any day I chose to prosecute you for writing such a letter." He said, " The letter was privileged, as it was written to my son." I said, " How dare you say such things to me about your son and me ? " He said, "You were both kicked out of the Savoy Hotel at a moment's notice for your disgusting conduct." I said, " That is a lie." He said, " You have taken furnished rooms for him in Piccadilly." I said, " Somebody has been telling you an absurd set of lies about your son and me. I have done nothing of the kind." He said, " I hear you were thoroughly well blackmailed for a disgusting letter you wrote to my son." I said, " The letter was a beautiful letter, and I never write except for publication." Then I asked : " Lord Queensberry, do you seriously accuse your son and me of improper conduct ? " He said, "I do not say that you are it, but you look it, as you pose as it, which is just as bad. If I catch you and my son together again in any public restaurant I will thrash you." I said, " I do not know what the Queensberry rules are, but the Oscar Wilde rule is to shoot at sight." I then told Lord Queensberry to leave my house.

* * *

Cross-examined by Edward Carson.

MR. CARSON :

You are of opinion, I believe, that there is no such thing as an immoral book ?

OSCAR WILDE :

Yes.

MR. CARSON:

May I take it that you think *The Priest and the Acolyte* was not immoral?

OSCAR WILDE:

It was worse; it was badly written.

* * *

Later in the cross-examination he was questioned about an article which appeared in " The Chameleon."

OSCAR WILDE:

I strongly objected to the whole story. I took no steps to express disapproval of *The Chameleon* because I think it would have been beneath my dignity as a man of letters to associate myself with an Oxford undergraduate's productions. I am aware that the magazine may have been circulated among the undergraduates of Oxford. I do not believe that any book or work of art ever had any effect whatever on morality.

MR. CARSON:

Am I right in saying that you do not consider the effect in creating morality or immorality?

OSCAR WILDE:

Certainly, I do not.

MR. CARSON:

So far as your works are concerned, you pose as not being concerned about morality or immorality?

OSCAR WILDE:

I do not know whether you use the word in any particular sense.

MR. CARSON:

It is a favourite word of your own.

OSCAR WILDE:

Is it? I have no pose in this matter. In writing a play or a book, I am concerned entirely with literature—that is, with art. I aim not at doing good or evil, but in trying to make a thing that will have some quality of beauty.

MR. CARSON:

Listen, sir. Here is one of the " Phrases and Philosophies for the Use of the Young " which you contributed: " Wickedness

226

is a myth invented by good people to account for the curious attractiveness of others." You think that true?

OSCAR WILDE:

I rarely think that anything I write is true.

MR. CARSON:

Did you say " rarely."

OSCAR WILDE:

I said "rarely." I might have said " never "—not true in the actual sense of the word.

MR. CARSON:

" Religions die when they are proved to be true." Is that true?

OSCAR WILDE:

Yes; I hold that. It is a suggestion towards a philosophy of the absorption of religions by science, but it is too big a question to go into now.

MR. CARSON:

Do you think that was a safe axiom to put forward for the philosophy of the young?

OSCAR WILDE:

Most stimulating.

MR. CARSON:

" If one tells the truth, one is sure sooner or later, to be found out " ?

OSCAR WILDE:

That is a pleasing paradox, but I do not set very high store on it as an axiom.

MR. CARSON:

Is it good for the young?

OSCAR WILDE:

Anything is good that stimulates thought in whatever age.

MR. CARSON:

Whether moral or immoral?

OSCAR WILDE:

There is no such thing as morality or immorality in thought. There is immoral emotion.

MR. CARSON:

" Pleasure is the only thing one should live for ? "

OSCAR WILDE :

I think that the realization of oneself is the prime aim of life, and to realize oneself through pleasure is finer than to do so through pain. I am, on that point, entirely on the side of the ancients—the Greeks. It is a pagan idea.

MR. CARSON :

" A truth ceases to be true when more than one person believes in it " ?

OSCAR WILDE :

Perfectly. That would be my metaphysical definition of truth; something so personal that the same truth could never be appreciated by two minds.

MR. CARSON :

" The condition of perfection is idleness : the aim of perfection is youth " ?

OSCAR WILDE :

Oh, yes; I think so. Half of it is true. The life of contemplation is the highest life, and so recognized by the philosopher.

MR. CARSON :

" There is something tragic about the enormous number of young men there are in England at the present moment who start life with perfect profiles, and end by adopting some useful profession " ?

OSCAR WILDE :

I should think that the young have enough sense of humour.

MR. CARSON :

You think that is humorous?

OSCAR WILDE :

I think it is an amusing paradox, an amusing play on words.

MR. CARSON :

What would anybody say would be the effect of *Phrases and Philosophies* taken in connection with such an article as *The Priest and the Acolyte* ?

OSCAR WILDE :

Undoubtedly it was the idea that might be formed that made me object so strongly to the story. I saw at once that maxims that were perfectly nonsensical, paradoxical, or anything you like, might be read in conjunction with it.

228

MR. CARSON:

This is in your introduction to *Dorian Gray:* "There is no such thing as a moral or an immoral book. Books are well written, or badly written." That expresses your view?

OSCAR WILDE:

My view on art, yes.

MR. CARSON:

Then, I take it, that no matter how immoral a book may be, if it is well written, it is, in your opinion, a good book?

OSCAR WILDE:

Yes, if it were well written so as to produce a sense of beauty, which is the highest sense of which a human being can be capable. If it were badly written, it would produce a sense of disgust.

MR. CARSON:

Then a well-written book putting forward perverted moral views may be a good book?

OSCAR WILDE:

No work of art ever puts forward views. Views belong to people who are not artists.

MR. CARSON:

A perverted novel might be a good book?

OSCAR WILDE:

I don't know what you mean by a " perverted " novel.

MR. CARSON:

Then I suggest *Dorian Gray* as open to the interpretation of being such a novel?

OSCAR WILDE:

That could only be to brutes and illiterates. The views of Philistines on art are incalculably stupid.

MR. CARSON:

An illiterate person reading *Dorian Gray* might consider it such a novel?

OSCAR WILDE:

The views of illiterates on art are unaccountable. I am concerned only with my view of art. I don't care tuppence what other people think of it.

229

MR. CARSON:

The majority of persons would come under your definition of Philistines and illiterates?

OSCAR WILDE:

I have found wonderful exceptions.

MR. CARSON:

Do you think that the majority of people live up to the position you are giving us?

OSCAR WILDE:

I am afraid they are not cultivated enough.

MR. CARSON:

Not cultivated enough to draw the distinction between a good book and a bad book?

OSCAR WILDE:

Certainly not.

MR. CARSON:

The affection and love of the artist of *Dorian Gray* might lead an ordinary individual to believe that it might have a certain tendency?

OSCAR WILDE:

I have no knowledge of the views of ordinary individuals.

MR. CARSON:

You did not prevent the ordinary individual from buying your book?

OSCAR WILDE:

I have never discouraged him.

* * *

Mr. Carson read passages from " Dorian Gray."

MR. CARSON:

Do you mean to say that that passage describes the natural feeling of one man towards another ?

OSCAR WILDE:

It would be the influence produced by a beautiful personality.

MR. CARSON:

A beautiful person?

OSCAR WILDE:

I said a " beautiful personality." You can describe it as you like. Dorian Gray's was a most remarkable personality.

230

MR. CARSON:

May I take it that you, as an artist, have never known the feeling described here?

OSCAR WILDE:

I have never allowed any personality to dominate my art.

MR. CARSON:

But let us go over it phrase by phrase. " I quite admit that I adored you madly." What do you say to that? Have you ever adored a young man madly?

OSCAR WILDE:

No, not madly; I prefer love—that is a higher form.

MR. CARSON:

Never mind about that. Let us keep down to the level we are at now.

OSCAR WILDE:

I have never given adoration to anybody except myself.

MR. CARSON:

I suppose you think that a very smart thing?

OSCAR WILDE:

Not at all.

MR. CARSON:

Then you have never had that feeling?

OSCAR WILDE:

No. The whole idea was borrowed from Shakespeare, I regret to say—yes, from Shakespeare's sonnets.

MR. CARSON:

I believe you have written an article to show that Shakespeare's sonnets were suggestive of unnatural vice?

OSCAR WILDE:

On the contrary I have written an article to show that they are not.*

MR. CARSON:

" I have adored you extravagantly." Do you mean financially?

OSCAR WILDE:

Oh, yes, financially.

* Portrait of Mr. W. H.

231

MR. CARSON:

Do you think we are talking about finance?

OSCAR WILDE:

I don't know what you are talking about.

MR. CARSON:

Don't you? Well, I hope I shall make myself very plain before I have done. " I was jealous of everyone to whom you spoke." Have you ever been jealous of a young man?

OSCAR WILDE:

Never in my life.

MR. CARSON:

" I wanted to have you all to myself." Did you ever have that feeling?

OSCAR WILDE:

No; I should consider it an intense nuisance, an intense bore.

MR. CARSON:

" I grew afraid that the world would know of my idolatry." Why should he grow afraid that the world should know of it?

OSCAR WILDE:

Because there are people in the world who cannot understand the intense devotion, affection, and admiration that an artist can feel for a wonderful and beautiful personality. These are the conditions under which we live. I regret them.

MR. CARSON:

In another passage Dorian Gray receives a book. Was the book to which you refer a moral book?

OSCAR WILDE:

Not well written, but it gave me an idea.

MR. CARSON:

Was not the book in mind of a certain tendency?

OSCAR WILDE:

I decline to be cross-examined upon the work of another artist. It is an impertinence and a vulgarity.

* * *

MR. CARSON:

These unfortunate people, that have not the high understanding that you have, might put it down to something wrong?

OSCAR WILDE:

Undoubtedly; to any point they chose. I am not concerned with the ignorance of others.

* * *

Mr. Carson read an extract from "The Picture of Dorian Gray" concerning the conversation between the artist, Basil Hallward, and Dorian Gray.

MR. CARSON:

Does not this passage suggest a charge of unnatural vice?

OSCAR WILDE:

It describes Dorian Gray as a man of very corrupt influence, though there is no statement as to the nature of the influence. But as a matter of fact I do not think that one person influences another, nor do I think there is any bad influence in the world.

MR. CARSON:

A man never corrupts a youth?

OSCAR WILDE:

I think not.

MR. CARSON:

Nothing would corrupt him?

OSCAR WILDE:

If you are talking of separate ages.

MR. CARSON:

No, sir, I am talking common sense.

OSCAR WILDE:

I do not think one person influences another.

MR. CARSON:

You don't think that flattering a young man, making love to him, in fact, would be likely to corrupt him?

OSCAR WILDE:

No.

Mr. Carson then referred to a letter written by Wilde to Lord Alfred Douglas.

MR. CARSON:

Where was Lord Alfred Douglas staying when you wrote that letter to him?

OSCAR WILDE :

At the Savoy; and I was at Babbacombe, near Torquay.

MR. CARSON :

It was a letter in answer to something he had sent you?

OSCAR WILDE :

Yes, a poem.

MR. CARSON :

Why should a man of your age address a boy nearly twenty years younger as " My own boy? "

OSCAR WILDE :

I was fond of him. I have always been fond of him.

MR. CARSON :

Do you adore him?

OSCAR WILDE :

No, but I have always liked him. I think it is a beautiful letter. It is a poem. I was not writing an ordinary letter. You might as well cross-examine me as to whether King Lear or a sonnet of Shakespeare was proper.

MR. CARSON :

Apart from art, Mr. Wilde?

OSCAR WILDE :

I cannot answer apart from art.

MR. CARSON :

Suppose a man who was not an artist had written this letter, would you say it was a proper letter?

OSCAR WILDE :

A man who was not an artist could not have written that letter.

MR. CARSON :

Why?

OSCAR WILDE :

Because nobody but an artist could write it. He certainly could not write the language unless he were a man of letters.

MR. CARSON :

I can suggest, for the sake of your reputation, that there is nothing very wonderful in this " red rose-leaf lips of yours " ?

OSCAR WILDE :

A great deal depends on the way it is read.

MR. CARSON:

"Your slim gilt soul walks between passion and poetry." Is that a beautiful phrase?

OSCAR WILDE:

Not as you read it, Mr. Carson. You read it very badly.

* * *

Later in the cross-examination.

MR. CARSON:

Did you become intimate with a young lad named Alphonse Conway at Worthing?

OSCAR WILDE:

Yes.

MR. CARSON:

He sold newspapers at the kiosk on the pier?

OSCAR WILDE:

No, I never heard that up to that time his only occupation was selling newspapers. It is the first I have heard of his connection with literature.

* * *

Mr. Carson questioned Wilde concerning his friendship with Charles Parker.

MR. CARSON:

What was there in common between this young man and yourself? What attraction had he for you?

OSCAR WILDE:

I delight in the society of people much younger than myself. I like those who may be called idle and careless. I recognize no social distinctions at all of any kind; and to me youth, the mere fact of youth, is so wonderful that I would sooner talk to a young man for half an hour than be—well, cross-examined in Court.

MR. CARSON:

Do I understand that even a young boy you might pick up in the street would be a pleasing companion?

OSCAR WILDE:

I would talk to a street arab, with pleasure.

MR. CARSON:

You would talk to a street arab?

235

OSCAR WILDE :
If he would talk to me.   Yes, with pleasure.

* * *

MR. CARSON :
Did Atkins call you " Oscar "?
OSCAR WILDE :
Yes.   I called him " Fred ", because I always call by their Christian names people whom I like.   People I dislike I call something else.

* * *

MR. CARSON :
Was he intellectual?   Was he an educated man?
OSCAR WILDE :
Culture was not his strong point.   He was not an artist. Education depends on what one's standard is.

* * *

MR. CARSON :
How much money did you give Parker?
OSCAR WILDE :
During the time I have known him I should think £4 or £5.
MR. CARSON :
Why?   For what reason?
OSCAR WILDE :
Because he was poor, and I liked him.   What better reason could I have?
MR. CARSON :
Did you ask what his previous occupation was?
OSCAR WILDE :
I never inquire about people's pasts.
MR. CARSON :
Nor their future?
OSCAR WILDE :
Oh, that is problematical.

236

MR. CARSON:

Did you know that one Parker was a gentleman's valet, and the other a groom?

OSCAR WILDE:

I did not know it, but if I had I should not have cared. I didn't care tuppence what they were. I liked them. I have a passion to civilize the community.

MR. CARSON:

What enjoyment was it to you to entertain grooms and coachmen?

OSCAR WILDE:

The pleasure to me was being with those who are young, bright, happy, careless, and free. I do not like the sensible and I do not like the old.

* * *

MR. CARSON:

Did Charles Parker call you " Oscar "?

OSCAR WILDE:

Yes. I like to be called " Oscar " or " Mr. Wilde ".

MR. CARSON:

You had wine?

OSCAR WILDE:

Of course.

MR. CARSON:

Was there plenty of champagne?

OSCAR WILDE:

Well, I did not press wine upon them.

MR. CARSON:

You did not stint them?

OSCAR WILDE:

What gentleman would stint his guests?

* * *

MR. CARSON:

Do you drink champagne yourself?

OSCAR WILDE:

Yes; iced champagne is a favourite drink of mine—strongly against my doctor's orders.

MR. CARSON:

Never mind your doctor's orders, sir.

OSCAR WILDE:

I never do.

*　　*　　*

MR. CARSON:

In March or April of last year did you go one night to visit Parker at 50 Park Walk, about half-past twelve at night.

OSCAR WILDE:

No.

MR. CARSON:

Is Park Walk about ten minutes walk from Tite Street?

OSCAR WILDE:

I don't know, I never walk.

MR. CARSON:

I suppose when you pay visits you always take a cab?

OSCAR WILDE:

Always.

MR. CARSON:

And if you visited, you would leave the cab outside?

OSCAR WILDE:

If it were a good cab.

*　　*　　*

Mr. Carson questioned Wilde about his acquaintance with a young man Fred Atkins.

MR. CARSON:

You dined with him?

OSCAR WILDE:

Yes.

MR. CARSON:

Gave him an excellent dinner?

OSCAR WILDE:

I never had anything else. I do everything excellently.

MR. CARSON:
Did you give him plenty of wine at dinner?

OSCAR WILDE:
As I have said before, anyone who dines at my table is not stinted in wine. If you mean, did I ply him with wine I say " No!" It's monstrous, and I won't have it.

MR. CARSON:
I have not suggested it.

OSCAR WILDE:
But you have suggested it before.

*   *   *

MR. CARSON:
You know a man named Ernest Scarfe?

OSCAR WILDE:
Yes. He was introduced to me by Taylor. He is a young man of about twenty, of no occupation. He had been in Australia at the gold-diggings.

MR. CARSON:
Did you know he was a valet and is a valet still?

OSCAR WILDE:
No. I have never met him in Society, though he has been in my society, which is more important.

MR. CARSON:
Why did you ask him to dinner?

OSCAR WILDE:
Because I am so good-natured. It is a good action to ask to dinner those beneath one in social station.

Cross-examination. The First Trial.

239

THE SECOND TRIAL

Mr. C. F. Gill :

You are acquainted with a publication entitled *The Chameleon*?

Oscar Wilde :

Very well indeed.

Mr. C. F. Gill :

Contributors to that journal are friends of yours?

Oscar Wilde :

That is so.

Mr. C. F. Gill :

I believe that Lord Alfred Douglas was a frequent contributor?

Oscar Wilde :

Hardly that, I think. He wrote verses occasionally for *The Chameleon,* and indeed for other papers.

Mr. C. F. Gill :

The poems in question were somewhat peculiar?

Oscar Wilde :

They were certainly not mere commonplaces like so much that is labelled poetry.

Mr. C. F. Gill :

The tone of them met with your critical approval?

Oscar Wilde :

It was not for me to approve or disapprove. I left that to the reviews.

* * *

Mr. C. F. Gill :

What is the " Love that dare not speak its name "?

Oscar Wilde :

" The Love that dare not speak its name " in this century is such a great affection of an elder for a younger man as there was between David and Jonathan, such as Plato made the very basis of his philosophy, and such as you find in the sonnets of

240

Michelangelo and Shakespeare. It is that deep, spiritual affection that is as pure as it is perfect. It dictates and pervades great works of art like those of Shakespeare and Michelangelo, and those two letters of mine, such as they are. It is in this century misunderstood, so much misunderstood that it may be described as the " Love that dare not speak its name ", and on account of it I am placed where I am now. It is beautiful, it is fine, it is the noblest form of affection. There is nothing un-natural about it. It is intellectual, and it repeatedly exists between an elder and a younger man, when the elder man has intellect, and the younger man has all the joy, hope and glamour of life before him. That it should be so the world does not understand. The world mocks at it and sometimes puts one in the pillory for it.

*   *   *

MR. C. F. GILL :
I wish to call your attention to the style of your correspondence with Lord Alfred Douglas?
OSCAR WILDE :
I am ready. I am never ashamed of the style of my writings.
MR. C. F. GILL :
Do you think an ordinarily constituted being would address such expressions to a younger man?
OSCAR WILDE :
I am not happily, I think, an ordinarily constituted being.

*   *   *

MR. C. F. GILL :
Not the sort of street you would usually visit in? You had not other friends there?
OSCAR WILDE :
No; this was merely a bachelor's place.
MR. C. F. GILL :
Rather a rough neighbourhood?
OSCAR WILDE :
That I don't know. I know it was near the Houses of Parliament.

Mr. C. F. Gill:

You made handsome presents to all these young fellows?

Oscar Wilde:

Pardon me, I differ. I gave two or three of them a cigarette case. Boys of that class smoke a good deal of cigarettes. I have a weakness for presenting my acquaintances with cigarette cases.

Mr. C. F. Gill:

Rather an expensive habit if indulged in indiscriminately, isn't it?

Oscar Wilde:

Less extravagant than giving jewelled garters to ladies.

XLVIII

PRISON

Wilde suffered in full the barbarities and indignities of prison life, the solitary confinement, the plank bed, and the squalor. He picked oakum, turned the crank, and cleaned out his cell, with the rest. In eighteen months, at Wandsworth and then at Reading Gaol, he endured the horrors and harsh treatment, until during the last six months of his sentence, the Governor of Reading Gaol was changed and the punishment of the prisoners relaxed. Wilde was allowed to write and during these last months " De Profundis " was written in the form of a letter to Lord Alfred Douglas.

Whilst in prison, Oscar Wilde wrote, that everything about his tragedy had been hideous and mean, and described how on 13th November, 1895, he was transferred from Wandsworth to Reading Gaol. On that day, during the afternoon, he had to stand on the centre platform of Clapham Junction in convict dress, handcuffed, for all the world to see. He was the object of ridicule and laughter, and with each train load the jeering audience grew. That was before they knew who he was. When they learned that the grotesque figure in prison garb was Oscar Wilde they laughed even louder.

Wilde was visited in prison by an old friend who said that he did not believe a single word of the allegations against him, and that he believed Oscar to be the victim of a malicious plot. Wilde was touched by the trust and sympathy of his friend and burst into tears. He said, however, that although parts of the charges were untrue it was a fact that his life had been full of perverse pleasures, and that unless his friend accepted the full implications of this statement they could not be friends any more.

Wilde records that this came as a terrible shock to his friend who was forced to accept the unpalatable truth, but that they were still friends, and that he had not got his friendship on false pretences.

243

Efforts were made to have Wilde's sentence reduced but the appeal failed, and he served the full sentence. Later he was able to say that society's sending him to prison ranked with his father's sending him to Oxford, as a turning point in his life.

*

I don't think I shall ever write again. Something is killed in me. I feel no desire to write—I am unconscious of power. Of course my first year in prison destroyed me body and soul. It could not be otherwise.   *Letter from Paris, August 1898.*

*

I have the horror of death with the still greater horror of living.
Letter to Robert Ross from Reading Gaol, March 10th, 1896.

*

Even if I get out of this loathsome place I know there is nothing for me but a life of a pariah, of disgrace and penury and contempt.   *Letter to Robert Ross from Reading Gaol, undated.*

*

The refusal to commute my sentence has been like a blow from a leaden sword. I am dazed with a dull sense of pain. I had fed on hope and now anguish grown hungry feeds her fill on *me* as though she had been starved of her proper appetite. There are, however, kinder elements in this evil prison air than were before; sympathies have been shown to me and I no longer feel entirely isolated from humane influences which was before a source of terror and trouble to me, and I read Dante and make excerpts and notes for the pleasure of using a pen and ink . . . and I am going to take up the study of German. Indeed this seems to be the proper place for such a study.
Letter to Robert Ross from Reading Gaol, undated.

*

Prison life makes one see people and things as they really are. That is why it turns one to stone.
Letter to Robert Ross writen from Reading Prison.

In Wandsworth Gaol:
I could be patient, for patience is a virtue. It is not patience, it is apathy you want here, and apathy is a vice.

In Conversation.

*

To a convict who thought the prison was haunted by ghosts:
Not necessarily so. You see, prisons have no ancient tradition to keep up. You must go to some castle to see ghosts, where they are inherited along with the family jewels!

In Conversation.

*

On the books he read in prison:
I read Dante every day, in Italian, and all through . . . It was his *Inferno* above all that I read; how could I help liking it? Cannot you guess? Hell, we were in it—Hell, that was prison.

In Conversation.

*

Note to a Warder in Reading Gaol:
I hope to write about prison life and try to change it for others, but it is too terrible and ugly to make a work of art of. I have suffered too much in it to write plays about it.

*Written on the inside of an envelope
addressed to the Governor of Reading Gaol.*

*

Note to a Warder in Reading Gaol:
Please find out for me the name of A.2.11., also the names of the children who are in for the rabbits and the amount of the fine. Can I pay this and get them out? If so I will get them out tomorrow. Please, dear friend, do this for me. I must get them out! Think what a thing for me it would be to help three little children. I would be delighted beyond words. If I can do this by paying the fine tell the children they are to be released tomorrow by a friend and ask them to be happy and not tell anyone.

Written on odd fragment of paper.

245

When I was a boy my two favourite characters were Lucien de Rubempre and Julien Sorel. Lucien hanged himself, Julien died on the scaffold, and I died in prison.   *In Conversation.*

*

For romantic young people the world always looks best at a distance; and a prison where one's allowed to order one's own dinner is not at all a bad place.   *Vera, or The Nihilists.*

*

Prisoners are, as a class, extremely kind and sympathetic to each other. Suffering and the community of suffering makes people kind . . . In this, as in all other things, philanthropists and people of that kind are astray. It is not the prisoners who need reformation. It is the prisons.   *Letter to Daily Chronicle.*

*

I am not prepared to sit in the grotesque pillory they put me into, for all time : for the simple reason that I inherited from my father and my mother a name of high distinction in literature and art. . . . I don't defend my conduct, I explain it, also there are in the letter (*De Profundis*) certain passages which deal with my mental development in prison and the inevitable evolution of character and intellectual attitude toward life that has taken place, and I want you, and others who still stand by me and have affection for me, to know exactly in what mood and manner I hope to face the world. Of course, from one point of view I know that on the day of my release I shall be merely passing from one prison into another, and there are times when the whole world seems to me no larger than my cell and as full of terror for me. Still I believe that at the beginning God made a world for each separate man, and in that world, which is within us, one should seek to live.

> *This is an extract from a letter to Robert Ross from Reading Gaol, April 1st, 1897, which Wilde intended to accompany the manuscript of " De Profundis ", and in it he gave relevant instructions. The Governor refused to hand over the manuscript and Wilde gave it to Ross on his release in May 1897.*

I know that when plays last too long, spectators tire. My tragedy has lasted far too long; its climax is over; its end is mean; and I am quite conscious of the fact that when the end does come I shall return as an unwelcome visitant to a world that does not want me.

Letter to Robert Ross written from Reading Prison.

XLIX

O. W.

Oscar Wilde died on the 30th November 1900 of cerebral meningitis. During his illness he suffered agonizingly painful headaches and for long periods he was delirious and incoherent.

The letter included in this chapter, addressed to Robert Ross, is the last he sent before his death. Wilde's sense of humour is here exemplified, for even during his last illness it did not desert him. The letter was actually dictated on his death-bed when he was too ill to write himself, and was written down by his friend Maurice. The signature is in Wilde's own hand.

During his last illness he said that he was dying, as he had lived, beyond his means.

*

My name has two " O's ", two " F's " and two " W's ". A name which is destined to be in everybody's mouth must not be too long. It comes so expensive in the advertisements. When one is unknown, a number of Christian names are useful, perhaps needful. As one becomes famous, one sheds some of them, just as a balloonist, when rising higher, sheds unnecessary ballast . . . All but two of my five names have already been thrown overboard. Soon I shall discard another and be known simply as " The Wilde " or " The Oscar ".   *In Conversation.*

*

I'll be a poet, a writer, a dramatist, somehow or other I'll be famous, and if not famous I'll be notorious. Or perhaps . . .I'll rest and do nothing . . . These things are on the knees of the Gods. What will be, will be.   *In Conversation at Oxford.*

*

We watch ourselves, and the mere wonder of the spectacle enthralls us, and I am the only person in the world I should like to know thoroughly, but I don't see any chance of it just at present.   *In Conversation.*

248

I do not write to please cliques. I write to please myself.

In an Interview.

*

The only writers who have influenced me are Keats, Flaubert and Walter Pater, and before I came across them I had already gone more than half-way to meet them.   *In Conversation.*

*

Praise makes me humble, but when I am abused I know I have touched the stars.   *In Conversation.*

*

I have the simplest tastes. I am always satisfied with the best.

In Conversation (After Prison).

*

It is sad. One half of the world does not believe in God, and the other half does not believe in me.   *In Conversation.*

*

How could I have written to you during the last three months considering that I have been in bed since last Monday? I am very ill and the doctor is making all kinds of experiments. My throat is a limekiln, my brain a furnace and my nerves a coil of angry adders.

I am apparently in much the same state as yourself.

Maurice—you remember Maurice—has kindly come to see me and I've shared all my medicines with him and shown him what little hospitality I can. We are both horrified to hear that Bosie's suspicions of you are quite justified. That and your being a Protestant make you terribly *unique* (I have told Maurice how to spell the last word as I am afraid that he might have used a word which often occurs in the Protestant bible).

Alec lunched with Bosie and me one day and I lunched alone with him another. He was most friendly and pleasant and gave me a depressing account of you. I see that you like myself have become a *neurasthenic*. I have been so for four months quite unable to get out of bed till the afternoon, quite unable to write letters of any kind.   My doctor has been trying to cure me with arsenic and strychnine but without much success as I became poisoned through mussels.   So you see what an exacting and tragic life I have been leading.   Poisoning by mussels is very painful and when one has one's bath one looks like a leopard.   Pray never eat mussels.

As soon as I get well I'll write you a long letter.

The last letter from Hotel d'Alsace,
Rue des Beaux Arts, PARIS.
Wednesday (November, 1900).

BRIEF BIBLIOGRAPHY OF OSCAR WILDE

NOTE : *Letters to the Press and to friends, of general interest, are included in this list.*

Whilst the many articles and reviews written for periodicals are not mentioned in detail, the date of the first contribution to each periodical is indicated.

BIBLIOGRAPHY

CHORUS OF CLOUD MAIDENS; a poem adapted from Aristophanes. *The Dublin University Magazine,* November, 1875.

FROM SPRING DAYS TO WINTER; a poem. *The Dublin University Magazine,* January, 1876.

GRAFFITI D'ITALIA. I. SAN MINIATO; a poem. *The Dublin University Magazine,* March, 1876.

THE DOLE OF THE KING'S DAUGHTER; a poem. *The Dublin University Magazine,* June, 1876 (revised 1881).

THE TRUE KNOWLEDGE. *The Irish Monthly,* September, 1876.

LA BELLA DONNA DELLA MIA MENTE; a poem. *Kottabos,* 1876 (revised 1881).

ROME UNVISITED; a poem. *The Month and Catholic Review,* September, 1876. Published under the title of GRAFFITI D'ITALIA.

THE ROSE OF LOVE WITH A ROSE'S THORN; a poem. *Kottabos,* October, 1876.

WASTED DAYS; a poem. *Kottabos,* Michaelmas Term, 1877.

A FRAGMENT FROM THE AGAMEMNON OF AESCHYLUS—A NIGHT VISION. *Kottabos,* Hilary Term, 1877.

IMPRESSION: LE RÉVEILLON; a poem. *The Irish Monthly,* February, 1877. Published as LOTUS LEAVES.

IMPRESSIONS II: LA FUITE DE LA LUNE; a poem. *The Irish Monthly,* February, 1877. Published as Part III of LOTUS LEAVES.

SALVE SATURNIA TELLUS; a poem. *The Irish Monthly,* June, 1877 (revised 1881 under the title, SONNET ON APPROACHING ITALY).

URBS SACRA AETERNA; a sonnet. *The Illustrated Monitor,* June, 1877.

THE TOMB OF KEATS; an article. THE GRAVE OF KEATS; a sonnet. *The Irish Monthly,* July, 1877. (THE GRAVE OF KEATS, published as HEU MISERANDE PUER).

SONNET WRITTEN DURING HOLY WEEK AT GENOA. *The Illustrated Monitor,* July, 1877.

253

THE GROSVENOR GALLERY; an article. *The Dublin University Magazine*, July, 1877.

VITA NUOVA; a sonnet. *The Irish Monthly*, December, 1877 (revised 1881).

MAGDALEN WALKS; a poem. *The Irish Monthly*, April, 1878.

AVE MARIA GRATIA PLENA; a poem. *The Irish Monthly*, July, 1878.

RAVENNA; a poem. *Thos. Shrimpton & Son*, Oxford, July, 1878. (Newdigate Prize poem. Recited by Oscar Wilde in the Sheldonian Theatre, Oxford, June 26th, 1878).

LA BELLE MARGUERITE; a ballad. *Kottabos*, Hilary Term, 1879.

ATHANASIA; a poem. *Time*, April, 1879. Published as THE CONQUEROR OF TIME.

PHÈDRE; a sonnet to Sarah Bernhardt. *The World*, June, 1879.

EASTER DAY; a sonnet. *Waifs and Strays*, June, 1879.

THE NEW HELEN; a poem. *Time*, July, 1879 (revised 1881).

QUEEN HENRIETTA MARIA, CHARLES I, ACT III. *The World*, July, 1879.

SEN ARTYSTY; or THE ARTIST'S DREAM, by *Madam Helena Modjeska*. Translated from the Polish by *Oscar Wilde* (?). *Ruthledge's Christmas Annual*, 1880.

PORTIA; a sonnet. *The World*, January, 1880.

IMPRESSION DE VOYAGE; a poem. *Waifs and Strays*, March, 1880.

AVE IMPERATRIX; a poem on England. *The World*, August, 1880.

VERA; or THE NIHILISTS, a Drama in a Prologue and Four Acts. *Ranken & Co.*, London, September, 1880.

A VILLANELLE; a poem. *Pan*, September, 1880.

LIBERATIS SACRA FAMES; a sonnet. *The World*, November, 1880.

SERENADE (for Music); a sonnet. *Pan*, January, 1881. Published as TO HELEN (SERENADE OF PARIS).

IMPRESSION DU MATIN; a poem. *The World*, March, 1881.

IMPRESSIONS: I. LES SILHOUETTES. II. LA FUITE DE LA LUNE. *Pan*, April, 1881.

POEMS. *David Bogue,* London, June, 1881. Collection of all Wilde's poems to date with the following not previously published :—

SONNET TO LIBERTY, MILTON, LOUIS NAPOLÉON, SONNET ON THE MASSACRE OF THE CHRISTIANS IN BULGARIA, QUANTUM MUTATA, THEORETIKOS, THE GARDEN OF EROS, REQUIESCAT, ITALIA, SONNET ON HEARING THE DIES IRAE SUNG IN THE SISTINE CHAPEL, E TENBRIS, THE BURDEN OF ITYS, ENDYMION, AMOR INTELLEC-TUALIS, SANTA DECCA, THE GRAVE OF SHELLEY, FABIEN DEI FRANCHI, CAMMA, PANTHEA, AT VERONA, APOLOGIA, QUIA MULTUM AMAVI, SILENTIUM AMORIS, HER VOICE, MY VOICE, TAEDIUM VITAE, HUMANITAD.

UNDER THE BALCONY; a poem. *Shakespearean Show Book,* London, May, 1884.

Began writing articles for the *Pall Mall Gazette,* October 14, 1884.

IMPRESSIONS DE PARIS; a poem. *In a Good Cause,* November, 1885.

Began writing articles for the *Dramatic Review,* March 14, 1885.

Began writing articles for the *Nineteenth Century,* May, 1885.

Began writing articles for *Society,* July 4, 1885.

THE CANTERVILLE GHOST. *The Court and Society Review,* February, 1887; March, 1887.

THE SPHINX WITHOUT A SECRET. *The World,* April, 1887.

Began writing articles for the *Saturday Review,* May 7, 1887.

LORD ARTHUR SAVILE'S CRIME. *The Court and Society Review,* May, 1887.

Assumed Editorship of *Woman's World* (afterwards a regular contributor), June, 1887.

THE MODEL MILLIONAIRE. *The World,* June, 1887.

Began writing articles for *The Lady's Pictorial,* December, 1887.

THE HAPPY PRINCE AND OTHER TALES (THE HAPPY PRINCE, THE NIGHTINGALE AND THE ROSE, THE SELFISH GIANT, THE DEVOTED FRIEND, THE REMARKABLE ROCKET). *David Nutt,* May, 1888.

PEN, PENCIL AND POISON. *The Fortnightly Review,* January, 1889.

THE DECAY OF LYING. *The Nineteenth Century,* January, 1889.

SYMPHONY IN YELLOW; a poem. *Centennial Magazine,* February, 1889.

THE BIRTHDAY OF THE INFANTA. *Paris Illustre*, March, 1889.

THE PORTRAIT OF MR. W. H. *Blackwood's Edinburgh Magazine*, July, 1889.

TO THE FOREST; a poem. *The Lady's Pictorial*, December, 1889.

Began writing reviews for *The Speaker*, February 6, 1890.

THE PICTURE OF DORIAN GRAY; a novel. *Lippincott's Monthly Magazine*, June, 1890.

CORRESPONDENCE begun between Wilde and critics of DORIAN GRAY in *The St. James's Gazette*, June 26, 1890.

THE TRUE FUNCTION AND VALUE OF CRITICISM; WITH SOME REMARKS ON THE IMPORTANCE OF DOING NOTHING. *The Nineteenth Century*, July, 1890 (afterwards published as THE CRITIC AS ARTIST, Part I).

CORRESPONDENCE between Wilde and critics of DORIAN GRAY carried on in *The Scots Observer*, July 12, 1890.

Second Part of THE TRUE FUNCTION AND VALUE OF CRITICISM. *The Nineteenth Century*, September, 1890 (afterwards published as THE CRITIC AS ARTIST, Part II).

THE SOUL OF MAN UNDER SOCIALISM. *The Fortnightly Review*, February, 1891.

A PREFACE TO DORIAN GRAY. *The Fortnightly Review*, March, 1891.

THE PICTURE OF DORIAN GRAY (with preface and some chapters added). *Ward Lock*, April, 1891.

INTENTIONS (THE DECAY OF LYING, PEN, PENCIL AND POISON, THE CRITIC AS ARTIST, THE TRUTH ABOUT MASKS) all published before in periodicals. *James R. Osgood McIlvaine*, May, 1891.

LORD ARTHUR SAVILE'S CRIME AND OTHER STORIES (LORD ARTHUR SAVILE'S CRIME, THE SPHINX WITHOUT A SECRET, THE CANTERVILLE GHOST, THE MODEL MILLIONAIRE) all published before in periodicals. *James R. Osgood McIlvaine*, July, 1891.

A HOUSE OF POMEGRANATES (THE YOUNG KING, THE BIRTHDAY OF THE INFANTA [published before in periodicals], THE FISHERMAN AND HIS SOUL, THE STAR CHILD [published for the first time]). *James R. Osgood McIlvaine*, November, 1891.

THE NEW REMORSE; a sonnet. *The Spirit Lamp*, December, 1892.

THE HOUSE OF JUDGEMENT. *The Spirit Lamp,* February, 1893.

SALOMÉ. *Librairie de l'Art Independant,* Paris, February, 1893.

THE DISCIPLE. *The Spirit Lamp,* June, 1893.

LADY WINDERMERE'S FAN; a Play about a Good Woman. *Elkin Matthews and John Lane,* November, 1893.

SALOMÉ (translated from the French by Lord Alfred Douglas). *Elkin Matthews and John Lane,* February, 1894. Illustrated by Aubrey Beardsley.

THE SPHINX (with decorations by Charles Ricketts). *Elkin Matthews and John Lane,* June, 1894.

POEMS IN PROSE (THE ARTIST, THE DOER OF GOOD, THE DISCIPLE, THE MASTER, THE HOUSE OF JUDGEMENT, THE TEACHER OF WISDOM). *The Fortnightly Review,* July, 1894.

A WOMAN OF NO IMPORTANCE; a play. *John Lane,* October, 1894.

PHRASES AND PHILOSOPHIES FOR THE USE OF THE YOUNG. *The Chameleon,* December, 1894.

THE CASE OF WARDER MARTIN, SOME CRUELTIES OF PRISON LIFE; a letter. *The Daily Chronicle,* May 28, 1897.

CHILDREN IN PRISON AND OTHER CRUELTIES. *Murdoch,* London, 1897.

THE BALLAD OF READING GAOL (by C.3.3.). *Leonard Smithers,* February, 1898.

DON'T READ THIS IF YOU WANT TO BE HAPPY TODAY; an article. *The Daily Chronicle,* March 24, 1898.

THE IMPORTANCE OF BEING EARNEST; A TRIVIAL COMEDY FOR SERIOUS PEOPLE. *Leonard Smithers,* February, 1899.

AN IDEAL HUSBAND; a play. *Leonard Smithers,* July, 1899.

AFTER READING. *The Beaumont Press,* 1921.

DE PROFUNDIS (abridged by Robert Ross). *Methuen,* February, 1905.

IMPRESSIONS OF AMERICA. *Keystone Press,* Sunderland, 1906.

DECORATIVE ART IN AMERICA. *Brentanos,* New York, 1906.

WILDE *v.* WHISTLER. Privately printed, London, 1906.

257

THE DUCHESS OF PADUA. *Methuen,* London, 1907. (Private printing, New York, 1883).

ART AND MORALITY. Edited by Stuart Mason (Reviews of DORIAN GRAY with replies by Wilde). *J. Jacobs,* London, 1908.

M.B.J. (Poem to Margaret Burne Jones). *John Rodker* private press, London, 1920.

CHARMIDES AND OTHER POEMS. *Methuen,* London, 1922.

AFTER BERNEVAL. *Beaumont Press,* 1922.

LETTERS TO THE SPHINX. *Duckworth,* London, 1930.

SIXTEEN LETTERS FROM OSCAR WILDE. *Faber & Faber,* 1930.

BOOKS CONSULTED.

The Works of Oscar Wilde. New Collected Edition, 1948, edited by G. F. Maine.

Oscar Wilde: A Study by P. Braybrook, 1930.

Oscar Wilde: The Man, The Artist, The Martyr. Boris Brazol, 1938.

Bernard Shaw, Frank Harris and Oscar Wilde. Robert H. Sherard, 1937.

Oscar Wilde and Myself. Lord Alfred Douglas, 1914.

The Life and Confessions of Oscar Wilde. Frank Harris, 1938, with Prefaces by George Bernard Shaw.

Echo de Paris. Laurence Houseman, 1923.

Oscar Wilde: A Summing Up. Lord Alfred Douglas, 1940.

Conversations with Oscar Wilde. A. H. C. Pritchard, 1931.

The Life of Oscar Wilde. Robert H. Sherard, 1906.

Bibliography of Oscar Wilde. Stuart Mason, 1914.

Aspects of Wilde. Vincent O'Sullivan, 1936.

The Real Oscar Wilde. Robert H. Sherard, 1915.

Time Was. W. Graham Robertson, 1938.

As We Were. E. F. Benson, 1930.

Oscar Wilde and the Yellow Nineties. Frances Winwar, 1940.

Oscar Wilde: Selected Works. Richard Aldington, 1946.

De Profundis. The Complete Text, with an Introduction by Vyvyan Holland, 1949.

Oscar Wilde: A Study. André Gide, 1905.

Men and Memories: Recollections of William Rothenstein. 1931.

The Life of Oscar Wilde. Hesketh Pearson, 1946.

Recollections of Oscar Wilde. Charles Ricketts, 1932.

The Aesthetic Movement in England. Walter Hamilton, 1882.

Oscar Wilde. G. J. Renier, 1933.

The Romantic 90's. Richard Le Gallienne, 1925.

Oscar Wilde Discovers America. Lloyd Lewis and Henry Justin Smith, 1936.

My Diaries. Wilfred Scawen Blunt, 1932.

Oscar Wilde, Fragments and Memories.   Martin Birnbaum, 1920.

Impressions of America.   Oscar Wilde, edited by Stuart Mason, 1906.

Oscar Wilde: Three Times Tried.   Compiled by Stuart Mason, 1912.

The Trials of Oscar Wilde.   Edited with an Introduction by H. Montgomery Hyde, 1948.

A Book of Famous Wits.   Walter Jerrold, 1912.

Oscar Wilde and the Black Douglas.   The Marquess of Queensberry in collaboration with Percy Colson, 1949.

Victorians, Edwardians and Georgians.   John Boon, Vol. I, 1928.

Memories of a Mis-spent Youth.   Grant Richards, 1932.

The Gentle Art of Making Enemies.   James McNeill Whistler, 1904.

Oscar Wilde: Some Reminiscences.   Leonard Cresswell Ingleby, 1907.

After Berneval: Letters from Oscar Wilde to Robert Ross.   1921.

After Reading: Letters from Oscar Wilde to Robert Ross.   1922.

The Paradox of Oscar Wilde.   George Woodcock, 1949.

Letters to the Sphinx from Oscar Wilde, with Reminiscences of the Author.   Ada Leverson, 1930.

Without Apology.   Lord Alfred Douglas, 1938.

Resurgam.   Unpublished Letters by Oscar Wilde, privately printed by Clement Shorter, 1917.

Oscar Wilde and the Theatre.   James Agate, 1947.

Oscar Wilde: A Retrospect.   E. P. Bentz, 1921.

Oscar Wilde.   L. F. Choisy, 1927.

Oscar Wilde.   Arthur Ransome, 1912.

Oscar Wilde, a Study of the Man and His Work.   R. Thurston Hopkins, 1913.

Oscar Wilde: the Story of an Unhappy Friendship.   R. H. Sherard, 1903.

A Study of Oscar Wilde.   Arthur Symons, 1930.

Selected Poems by Oscar Wilde.   With a Preface by Robert Ross, 1911.

Impressions of America.   Oscar Wilde, edited by Stuart Mason, 1906.